# Hand of Vengeance

This book is sold subject to the condition that it shall not, by way of trade or otherwise, be lent, resold, hired out or otherwise circulated without the author's and publisher's prior consent in any form. No part of this publication may be reproduced, stored in or introduced into a retrieval system or transmitted in any form or by any means (electronic, mechanical, photocopying, recording or otherwise) without the written permission of both the copyright owner and the publisher of this book.

All characters and situations are entirely fictitious and any resemblance to real people or incidents is entirely coincidental

© Marc Alexander

ISBN 978-1-909473-05-8

Text prepared by www.willowebooks.org.uk

# Hand of Vengeance

by

# Marc Alexander

Published by Willow Books

For Beatrice Gauld

# CHAPTER 1

A tumbleweed rolled down the only street of Paradise. From the deep shadow of the warped verandahs a score of men watched its erratic progress with bored eyes until it was lost to view, once more following the drought wind across the desert. The eyes swivelled to where a dust devil was performing a graceful dance opposite the Golden Gate saloon. Heat hung heavy over the town like a curse.

Along the trail that led to Paradise rode two men. The first had red-rimmed eyes, a trail beard and, like so many travellers who had come through the badlands, a dejected stoop. Only the Colt Peacemaker, strapped dangerously low on his thigh, suggested he could be a man of action.

His companion, astride a weary roan a few feet behind, had no gun. He was tall and bulky and, despite the desert sun, his face was pale. Blue-tinted glasses shielded his eyes and gave him a slightly sinister air. There was something about him which made one think of a baby who had suddenly grown into a middle-aged man without the hardening process of early manhood.

The first traveller opened his dry mouth and cursed the sun and the sand and the wind which caressed him like the breath of a furnace.

'Goddam it, Professor,' he growled to the man behind, 'when we reach Paradise I aim to drink the town dry.'

'You'd better get that idea straight out of your head,' was the quiet reply. 'You hit the bottle too hard in

Bitter Springs, remember? Do it again and you'll end up on a one-way ride to Boothill. Once a gunman starts getting liquored up it's the end. There's many a young *hombre* who would like the opportunity to be the man who beat Frankie Kelso to the draw. A few drinks and you'll be giving 'em every chance.'

Frankie Kelso rubbed the tips of his fingers through his stubble and squinted blankly at the distant outline of Paradise.

'Maybe I'm gettin' past it,' he mumbled. 'I feel so goddam tired, Professor...tired of practisin' every day, tired of ridin' the circuit, tired of killin' my thirst with mineral water...an', most of all, tired of wonderin' where the next bullet's gonna come from.'

'If folks could hear that, they wouldn't believe it,' said the Professor, kicking the roan until it was alongside Kelso's mount. 'That ain't the way for the fastest gun in the State to talk. Why, man, you're Frankie Kelso. Everywhere you go folk know you, an' fear you. Even in the East your name is known...'

'Thanks to you.'

'An' all the pickings are yours. You're King, Frankie, just like Hickok or Ringo or Bonney.'

'Yeah, I guess you're right. I don't know what's wrong with me. At first I enjoyed it – I guess I was sick with fear, but I *enjoyed* it. Now I ain't scared no more, but somethin's gone...'

'It's the badlands,' said the Professor soothingly. 'They're mean an' they made you feel mean an' small. In Paradise, in your city clothes an' a deck of cards in front of you, you'll be King again, not just a thirsty saddletramp.'

Kelso opened his mouth to say something, then thought better of it. His lips compressed to a grim scar, he realised he had talked too much. That was the trouble, he couldn't keep anything back from the Professor.

Unconsciously his hand brushed against the walnut butt of the Colt .45, the gun with which he had blasted his way to fame. The Professor noticed the action and behind his blue spectacles his eyes narrowed.

Paradise seemed to swim towards them through the heat haze like a town in a mirage. Suddenly they were jingling down the main street towards the Golden Gate, while under the verandahs the watchers suddenly leaned forward. The arrival of strangers was always a break in the monotony, but when one of those strangers was Frankie Kelso...

An old man left the shade of the grain store and limped off to warn the marshal.

The odd couple, the flabby, baby-faced giant and the lean wolfish gun-fighter, turned their horses over to the liveryman at the Paradise Corral and walked stiffly into the Golden Gate.

The barkeep jerked to attention at the sight of customers.

'Name your poison, gents,' he said cheerfully, and then his smile faded as he noticed the cutaway holster on Kelso's thigh. He looked up at him, blinking in the hot gloom.

'Why, ain't you...?' he began.

'That's right,' said the Professor. 'Now, Mister Kelso would like a nice private room, *upstairs*. An' we'd both like to wash off this trail dirt...'

'But first Mister Kelso would like a drink,' said the gunfighter lounging against the bar. 'Gimme that bottle of Old Vermont, I got some alkali to clear from my throat.'

'Anything you say, yes siree, Mister Kelso,' said the barman, pushing the bottle across the counter.

'Thanks, pal,' said Kelso. He gave the Professor a slow, humourless smile and walked over to a table in the far corner.

'Pour me one, too,' said the Professor, towering above him. 'An' then listen to what I'm going to say.'

Kelso proffered him a glass, then drained his own. He wiped his mouth on the back of his sun-tanned hand.

'Now, don't preach to me, Professor,' he said, wincing a little as the raw spirit burned his throat. 'I reckon I got my loop round everythin' you're gonna say. You'll tell me a gunfighter has to stick to mineral water 'cause even one slug of Red Eye'll slow his reflexes...you'll tell me I gotta be dedicated, that I can't live like other men, that I'm somethin' special...Well, save yourself the breath. Today I'm gonna have myself a time an' to hell with my reflexes...there ain't anyone in this rat town I'd be scared of if I was blind drunk.'

'Listen, Kelso,' hissed the Professor suddenly leaning forward, 'you smell of death. If I hadn't hustled you out of Bitter Springs when I did, some young punk'd be wearing your gun now. You've begun to act loco, an' it's a stupid shame after all I...'

'Finish it, Professor,' said Kelso in a strangely quiet voice.

'Forget it,' said the Professor straightening up. 'I'm going out for a while.'

'Gonna look for the telegraph office?' asked Kelso with a sneer.

\* \* \*

'Come on, Saul, you've got to say your promise,' said the thin woman with the fanatical eyes.

'Aw, Ma, I wanna go out'n' play,' said the boy.

The woman stood in the doorway of the mean shack, the glare of the sun outside turning her into a tall silhouette. 'You don't budge till you've said it proper,' she said. 'One day you'll understand why – one day you'll thank me...now, say it.'

The tow-haired boy shuffled his bare toes in the

dust. He was about ten years old and, no doubt taking after his mother, was thin and wiry. But while her eyes were dark and smouldering with a strange, inner passion, his were a brilliant blue.

'All right, Ma, I'll say it,' he said resignedly.

'Good boy,' she said. From the wall she took down an old Volcanic rifle. 'Begin.'

'I, Saul Powers, swear on the gun of my father that when I – when I am a man I – I shall – shall...'

'Seek vengeance.'

'Seek vengeance on those who – who...'

'Murdered.'

'Murdered him. I shall not rest until I have sought out and slain...' The boy paused to draw a deep breath and then, as some children rattle off the final part of their prayers, cried: 'LewO'HaraBenRockwellCharlieGideonJesseNathanandtheCochiseKid – an' now can I go out an' play?'

'Amen to that,' said the mother. She sighed and replaced the Volcanic on the wall. 'Yes, you can go now.'

'Thanks, Ma.' The boy darted forward, then stopped abruptly when he saw a stranger at the door. He squinted up at him, fascinated by his blue-tinted spectacles.

'Hello, son,' he said gently. 'Is your Ma about?'

She came to the door, looking at the tall flabby man with deep suspicion.

'Am I addressing Mrs Powers, Mrs Luke Powers?'

'That's my name and it's one I ain't ashamed on.'

'Indeed, if your husband was the great Luke Powers, you should be very proud, ma'am. He had a fine – ah – reputation.'

For a moment Mrs Powers relaxed enough to smile, then she snapped: 'So what do you want with a poor widow woman?'

'I must explain. My name is Jonathan Coffin...'

'Say, that's a durn unlucky-soundin' name,' interjected Mrs Powers.

Jonathan Coffin smiled without humour.

'My friends call me "The Professor",' he said. 'I once had the honour of teaching English at an Academy for Young Ladies in Boston. Unfortunately...well, we need not go into it now, suffice to say I now represent a New York publishing house...'

'You a newspaper man?'

'You could call me a journalist, I suppose... I provide entertainment and instruction for thousands of readers back East. Second hand I give them the thrill of this pioneer land which they have not the stomach for themselves.'

'I get you,' said Mrs Powers. 'You want to write about my Luke.'

Professor Coffin nodded.

'Come in,' she said. 'I've got plenty to tell...Go an' play, Saul.'

Reluctantly the boy went off and stood watching a gang of boys playing with wooden guns. Mrs Powers would have been happier if he had joined in the game.

* * *

The sun, having turned Paradise into a hell during the day, slipped behind the horizon in a burst of glory. The sky became flame red, royal purple and then a soft indigo. A cool breeze suddenly sighed from nowhere and dark shadows raced across the desert plain. As night engulfed the world the yellow glow of kerosene lamps began to illuminate the windows of Paradise. Brightest lit was the Golden Gate saloon. It was drawing customers as its lights attracted suicidal moths. Tonight was an important night and one the citizens of Paradise would be able to recount to each other through many a long, hot summer.

Frankie Kelso, the fastest gun in the State, was holding court in the Golden Gate. It was rumoured he had downed ten men in face-to-face duels; it was said he was so accurate he once shot a bluebottle off the nose of a sleeping drunk without disturbing him; it was whispered he was on his way to try conclusions with Hickok...

When the Professor entered the saloon he found it thronged, though the customers were unusually quiet. The bartender could not keep up with the orders for beers and rye and the proprietor was behind the counter helping him fill the foaming schooners. The cripple at the piano was doing his frantic best and the three rather jaded hostesses had eyes for nobody but Kelso.

He was sitting with his back to the wall, a card table before him ringed with players. Others stood around, waiting for someone to drop out. They did not mind too much if they lost, in fact they felt a little relieved if they did, for it was a cheap price to pay for being able to say – casually – for the rest of their lives: 'Frankie Kelso? Sure I knew him – played poker with him.'

Since the Professor had left him, Kelso had been shaved and now wore his city clothes of which he was childishly proud. His suit was rich and dark, his waistcoat was maroon silk crossed by a gleaming watchchain. On his head was a curly brimmed derby, and the only thing to spoil the sartorial effect was the heavy gun belt and the Colt which crumpled his right trouser leg.

The Professor noted he was in high good humour – and slightly drunk, but this did not seem to affect his card work. There were several miniature towers of dollar pieces before him. Kelso was a lucky gambler, perhaps because no-one seemed inclined to cheat him.

'I'm startin' to like this town after all, Professor,' cried the gunman when he saw his companion. He swept a number of coins towards him. 'The gentlemen here sure know how to lose their money like sports...'

The Professor bought a beer and sat close at a table without replying. His silence annoyed Kelso who murmured under his breath before dealing another hand. Meanwhile the Professor noticed a curious thing, all the customers of the Golden Gate, apart from Kelso, were unarmed. Apparently the checking in of firearms was a house rule.

At the end of the round a youth stood up so suddenly that his chair fell with a crash. At the noise Kelso's right hand jerked down to his Peacemaker, then relaxed.

'I'm out of the game, Mister,' said the youth. 'I'm cleaned out.'

'That's tough, kid,' grinned Kelso. 'But at least get yourself a drink.' As he spoke he flipped a silver dollar. The boy caught it by reflex action, then furiously threw it back on the table.

'I don't need your goddam charity,' he said, his cheeks burning.

Conversation faded. For a few moments the piano continued its honky-tonk tune, then it too faltered and died.

Calmly Kelso picked up the silver dollar and fingered it thoughtfully, though his eyes never left the youth's face. He, on the other hand, was at a loss. Having made his gesture, he did not know what to do next.

'Son,' said Kelso slowly, so slowly that every word seemed to hang in the air, 'you did a darn loco thing just then. If you had been awearing a gun they'd be carryin' you out now. I gave you this dollar as a kindness, but you saw fit to throw it back. Maybe you did that because you guessed I wouldn't shoot an unarmed punk like you, an' you could brag – after I'd gone – how you threw Frankie Kelso's money back in his face. Waal, son, I ain't gonna let you do that.'

He rose slowly to his feet, leaned across the table to the boy and then suddenly swung his open hand against his face. It made a report like a pistol shot.

The youth's eyes watered with the blow. The gunman sank back into his chair.

'Mebbe it's lucky for you, Kelso, I ain't got a gun,' the youth muttered. He turned and quit the saloon.

The conversation started again and the cripple renewed his attack on the keyboard as though it was responsible for his twisted spine.

'Who was that young cuss?' asked Kelso as the game resumed.

'That was Grant Hicks,' said the man who had taken his place. 'Guess he was afraid his Ma would whup his tail for losin' his month's roll.' There was a guffaw.

'Waal, this is a game for men, not boys,' said Kelso genially, picking up a fan of cards.

Sometime later a grizzled, middle-aged man entered the saloon and pushed his way to Kelso's table. A tarnished marshal's star was pinned to his shirt and there was a bone-handled Colt at his side.

'Mister Kelso,' he said, his voice a fraction high with nervousness.

'At your service, marshal,' grinned Kelso, and the Professor realised he had never seen him so good humoured. It was as though the rye was unlocking a new personality.

'I hope you ain't gonna take no offence, Mister Kelso, but we have a rule in Paradise about the wearin' of guns in the saloon. This ain't much of a town, but we likes to keep it peaceful.'

'You askin' me to hand over my gun?'

'Just that, Mister Kelso.'

The gunman regarded the marshal with the same expression he had worn when he spoke to Grant Hicks, his face blank but with a strange gleam in his eyes. Again the piano shuddered to a stop.

'It'd take a better man than you to take my hardware, marshal,' he said quietly.

There was a slight hiss of indrawn breath. The Professor rose to his feet and coughed. The marshal turned to him, grateful for this break in the tension.

'I think you may not realise what you are asking my friend to do,' said the Professor. 'You are not asking an ordinary cattleman or miner to give up his arms, you are asking a man who has had to live by his weapon and who has made enemies. Circumstances forced him to become a professional gunman – you know the reputation he has earned. There are many men who would like to seize that fame for themselves so that when they walked down the sidewalk people would whisper: "There goes the man who shot down Frankie Kelso..." But what stops them is that instrument of protection my friend wears in his holster. Take that from him and you are asking for his life. You must understand, marshal, that a top gun is not like other men. At any moment...'

'Aw, shut up,' snarled Kelso. 'I don't need you to talk for me...' There was a slur in his voice that had not been there before, the effect of the alcohol had reached his vocal cords. 'If the marshal wants my gun he's welcome to come an' get it, if not he'd better vamoose pronto an' make sure no chickens are bein' rustled. I guess that's about the size of him.'

The marshal swallowed and looked back to the Professor as though for help, but the Professor, his mouth a lipless line, had sunk back in his chair. For a moment the saloon waited, poised on the edge of calamity – or comedy. In spite of itself the marshal's tongue ran along his dry lips. He knew he was at the crossroads of his career.

He could either do his duty at the risk of death or walk away alive...and a branded coward.

Fear won. Without another word he turned and stumbled out into the night. A cruel shout of laughter exploded as the batwing doors slammed behind him.

'Say, Mister Kelso, how'd you like to be our marshal?' cried an old-timer.

A grin slid across Kelso's face and he raised a bottle of Old Vermont in triumph, taking a long pull before setting it down again. Of the laughing, joking crowd, only the Professor was aware of the tremor in Kelso's hand.

The men at the card table returned to their game, the piano began to bang and tinkle and a hostess squeezed beside the hero of the moment, laughing as he showed her his hand of cards.

Then everything happened very quickly. The doors sprang apart and Grant Hicks ran through, a gunbelt now round his waist. As some instinct made the Golden Gate patrons cower away from the line of fire, they noticed Kelso's hand mark still burned like a crimson birthmark on the youth's cheek.

'Now we're on equal terms, Kelso,' shouted Hicks. 'Draw.'

The hostess beside Kelso screamed so suddenly and so loud that for a fraction of a second his eyes flicked in her direction. Next instant he was climbing to his feet while his hand slapped against the walnut of the Peacemaker. But Hicks already had his gun out. There was a crash of shots. Kelso screamed and jerked like a marionette whose strings were plucked simultaneously. His gun exploded, but the .45 slug buried itself in the saloon floor. Hicks continued firing until all his chambers were empty. Black powder smoke filled the Golden Gate and the lamps dimmed until they were pale glimmers in an acrid fog.

As the smoke cleared the Professor saw that his companion was stretched across the card table. Little snakes of dark blood oozed from under him. The expression in his wide, glazing eyes was of extreme surprise.

\* \* \*

The Professor walked into the shack which served as the Paradise telegraphic office. Without a word he picked up a pad of blanks and began to print out the words he had rehearsed through the night.

THE GLORIOUS CAREER OF TOPGUN FRANKIE KELSO ENDED IN THE FRONTIER TOWN OF PARADISE IN A BLAZE OF GUNFIRE STOP RIDDLED BY BULLETS THIS HANDSOME KNIGHT OF THE PLAINS WHO HAS SO BOLDLY FOUGHT HIS WAY INTO THE GALLERY OF WESTERN HEROES DIED WITH THESE WORDS ON HIS LIPS QUOTE TELL MOTHER I WENT WITH MY BOOTS ON UNQUOTE TODAY THE WEST MOURNS...

When he had finished the Professor read through his work with satisfaction, striking out unessential words to save cost. Then he scribbled the address of a New York newspaper on the top and handed it to the man at the Morse key.

'Say, that's about the longest message I've ever seen,' said the operator, scanning the form. 'My, my, but you've written that real pretty. Guess Kelso would feel mighty fine if he could read that.'

'I always did him proud,' murmured the Professor.

The sensitive fingers of the operator began to tap out the story. When it was finished he looked up with a quizzical expression.

'Tell me one thing, Professor,' he said. 'What guy is gonna be your subject now?'

The Professor did not answer. He turned and walked out into the hot morning where Grant Hicks was waiting.

# CHAPTER 2

The Wells Fargo Concord coach rolled down the trail leaving a fine cloud of white dust suspended in the warm air. Inside the heads of eight of the nine passengers nodded drowsily in unison with the coach as it rocked on its leather thorough braces. The ninth passenger kept his intense blue eyes on the window as though hypnotised by the endless panorama of wasteland, with its backdrop of ragged mountains.

He was a bony youth of about seventeen or eighteen, with hair so bleached by the sun that it was almost pure white. Even jammed in the corner seat there was a hidden restlessness about him which had caused the other travellers to look at him more than once before the rhythmic monotony of the journey lulled them into uneasy torpor.

Several of the passengers were drummers, with their sample bags beneath their feet. There was a trio of hard-eyed cattlemen who wore their guns and stank of whisky, and a professional gambler in a New York suit and floral waistcoat. But they held no interest for Saul Powers. He felt excitement within himself like a tightly coiled spring, and as the landscape lurched past with its sparse clumps of chaparral and saguaros, he could hardly believe he was on the way towards fulfilling the ambition of his young life.

The Concord began to slow down as it approached a staging post. Almost before the wheels had ceased to turn a fresh team of horses was being led out while the passengers climbed stiffly down from the coach.

'You have five minutes exactly to get yourselves a beer,' called the driver, and he winked at the man who was riding shotgun with him. Led by the thirsty cattlemen, the passengers straggled over to a cabin which had a crude bar rigged up inside it. Saul noticed that a sawn-off, double-barrelled shotgun lay on the bar within easy reach of the fat, sweat-sheened barman. He guessed that all the men who manned these lonely outposts had to have their weapons within easy reach in case of surprise attack by Indians or desperadoes.

Although he was short of money, the white-haired boy could not resist the idea of cold beer. He pressed his only ten dollar bill into the hand of the barman who pushed a foaming glass towards him. He seemed so busy satisfying the thirsts of the passengers that he was neglecting to give change. No doubt, thought Saul, he'll give me my money once everyone has a drink.

The boy had just put down his empty glass when a sharp report sounded outside. It was the crack of the stage coach driver's whip summoning the passengers back. As soon as they heard it some turned to go, for one of the worst things a traveller could ever do was to keep a Wells Fargo waiting – others began to argue with the bartender about change. Again the whip cracked.

'Tarnation, it's only a few cents – keep it, and I hope it chokes you,' muttered the gambler, and he turned to go. The drummers followed suit.

It was then Saul saw through the shabby trick. The barman held back the change on purpose, hoping to keep most of it in the confusion following the summons to the coach. Greenhorns in particular would be afraid to stay and argue. Well, he wasn't going to act like a greenhorn.

'Where's my change, fella?' he demanded. 'I gave you a ten dollar bill.'

The barman looked at him with surprise on his

greasy features.

'What ten dollar bill?' he spluttered. 'You gave me a dollar – an' at this post beer is a dollar a bottle.'

'You musta made a mistake,' replied Saul.' All I had was a ten dollar bill, an' now you've got it.'

From outside there came another whip crack.

'Come on, son, don't argue the toss, you're keeping the stage waiting,' called one of the drummers from the door.

'Yeah, vamoose, kid,' said the barman, 'and don't try them tricks here again. I've met your sort before.'

'Look,' said Saul in an icy voice, 'you know durned well I gave you a ten dollar bill. I aim to stay here and get my change if I have to hold up a dozen stages.'

Outside a fluent string of cuss words floated from the enraged coach driver.

'God dammit, we ain't got all day,' he yelled at the passengers who were now clustered outside the cabin, watching with some amusement the argument going on between the barman and the thin tense youth.

'I'm asking you for the last time, mister,' Saul hissed. 'Shell out my change pronto.'

'And you can burn in hell first,' snarled the fat man. 'I don't aim to be tricked by a punk bandit like you. Git outa my bar.'

As he spoke Saul saw his pudgy hand sliding across the top of the counter to where the shotgun lay. In a flash the youth's hand streaked down to his thigh and came up again holding an old-style single-action Colt. The barman froze as he found himself looking into the unrelenting eye of the pistol.

'Now don't get any fancy ideas about shotguns,' Saul reproved in a low dangerous voice. 'You just keep your hands on the bar, mister, where I can see 'em.'

The onlookers watched slack-mouthed. Few had

seen a faster draw than this, and even the driver and shotgun, who had come over to collect their passengers by force if necessary, stood fascinated by the drama that was being enacted within.

'Now,' said the boy quietly, 'as I paid you ten dollars, I aim to have ten dollars' worth of liquor.'

The gun exploded. With a yowl of terror the barman dropped behind his bar, but the bullet was not aimed at him. It shattered an expensive bottle of brandy above his head. Broken glass and spirit rained down upon him. Cursing, he raised his head above the counter to an accompaniment of unsympathetic laughter. Calmly Saul moved the muzzle of his pistol slightly, cocked the hammer and fired again. A bottle of whisky exploded into fragments.

'Stop! Stop!' the bartender implored. 'You can't waste liquor like that.'

'Can't I?' Saul grinned. 'As I figure I paid for it, I guess I can do what I like.' The Colt crashed again and more whisky ran down the wall behind the bar.

'For God's sake, take your money and go!' cried the bartender in a defeated voice. He held out ten dollars in a trembling hand.

'You can have the beer on the house,' he added.

Saul took the money and with the gun still in his hand backed out of the cabin. Infuriated by his defeat, the barman's hand had begun to move again towards the shotgun, but before he could touch it a bullet sent it skidding away from him.

'That was mighty fine shooting, son,' said one of the cattlemen.

'If Pat Garrett hadn't killed him, I'd have said you were Billy the Kid Bonney,' chimed in another.

'It wasn't anythin' really,' said Saul, loading his smoking gun as he walked back to the Concord. 'I guess I just happened to take after my old man.'

'So who was your Dad?' asked the gambler.

'Luke Powers,' said the boy with a look of pride on his face.

'I'll be damned!' said the gambler. 'Let me shake you by the hand, boy. By the look of you you're going to begin where he left off.'

\* \* \*

Dead on time, the Concord rolled into the old town of Juanita. Among the small crowd that surged forward to meet it from the shade of the old Spanish-style buildings was a tall flabby man with blue tinted spectacles. His mouth curled slightly in a humourless smile of satisfaction when he saw the slim form of Saul Powers descend from the stage and walk stiffly towards him.

'Hello, boy,' he said, 'I'm Professor Jonathan Coffin.'

Saul looked up at him.

'I remember you,' he said. 'I remember the day you came to see my Ma. It was the same day that Frankie Kelso was gunned down by Grant Hicks.'

'Well, that's old history now,' said the Professor. 'Right now we've got to look forward to the future. I'm renting an old place outside town. We can talk about my plans when we get out there.' He led Saul over to a hitching rail where he had a couple of mounts waiting.

As they rode out of Juanita, Saul felt embarrassed, not knowing what to say to the man he knew to be his benefactor. The Professor rode slightly ahead, not bothering to talk. At one stage, feeling he should say something, Saul murmured: 'I'd like to thank you, Professor, for the money you sent to my Ma. Things have been kinda tough with her for a long time now, an' I wasn't able to earn much back in Paradise.'

The Professor acknowledged this with a slight

shrug, still not saying anything. Clearly his mind was on something else. Before long they reached a ramshackle house. Many hot summers had passed since it had known the lick of a paint brush, its wooden shingles were curled, but it had the advantage of having no neighbours.

'Look after the horses, boy,' said the Professor, 'and I'll go inside and start cooking supper. Then you and I have got to have a long talk.'

When the meal was over the older man said: 'Now tell me, boy, what do you remember of your father's murder?'

'I was 'bout five years old,' Saul answered quietly. 'Yet I can see it like it was happenin' now. We were livin' in a pretty good house in them days. I guess with Dad being a pretty big peace officer an' all we weren't tight on money. I was just a shaver then, and that mornin' I was playin' on the verandah. I looked up when I heard the sound of horses. Five men rode up. My father went across the yard towards them. "Hello, boys," he said, but before he could do anything, they had pulled out their guns and began to fire at him.

'He was hit bad right away. He tried to go for his gun but before he could get it free he was lying in the dust. I can still hear him yellin' out: "Mary! Mary!" to my mother. She ran out of the door and when she saw him lying there she started screamin'.

'The men didn't say anything, they just bolstered their guns and rode away. By the time my Ma was bending over Dad he was dead. There was a terrible lot of blood because it seemed each man had emptied his gun into him. I was so surprised by it all that I didn't even holler.

'Though I was only a kid I knew my father was the greatest gunfighter in the district, which I guess is why the association of local ranchers'd made him peace officer. Lookin' back on it, I guess the thing that horrified me the most was that he had been shot down so easily. If only he could have got his gun out and killed a couple of the band I'd have felt better. But he never had a chance.'

Saul raised his eyes from the table. In the soft yellow light of the kerosene lamp he saw that the Professor had been making notes in a leather-backed 'You know who these men were?' asked the Professor.

'Yeah,' Saul nodded, 'My Ma used to make me repeat their names every day since the funeral. She knew when I'd be old enough I'd want to revenge myself for what they did. Their names were Lew O'Hara, Ben Rockwell, Charlie Gideon, Jesse Nathan and a fella called the Cochise Kid. I guess nobody knows what his real name was.'

'Did you have any notion as to why they would want to kill your Pa?' asked the Professor.

Saul shrugged. 'I figure they must have been a gang of rustlers,' he said. 'I guess Pa was makin' life too difficult for them, so they just came and got rid of him.'

'Had anyone else tried to shoot him?' asked the Professor.

'I don't rightly remember,' Saul replied, 'but according to my Mother there were a couple of attempts. Each time he was too quick on the draw. Certainly there hadn't been an attack like this. I guess he wasn't even aware of the danger until it was too late. They just shot him down like a dog. Well, sir, my day will come and each one of those men is going to die like a dog.'

'Amen to that,' said the Professor. 'Get rested now after your journey and tomorrow morning we'll see how handy you are with a gun. Once I reckon you're ready, we'll go after the first of those men – Lew O'Hara.'

'Do you know where he is then?' demanded Saul.

The Professor gave him a thin lipless smile. 'I sure do, boy,' he said. 'It took some tracking down, but I know where we can find him.'

Saul Powers' blue eyes glittered. 'Can we start right away?'

'Not yet. But don't fret none about that. You'll be meeting him soon enough. Now get some sleep. There's some real hard work ahead of you.'

'There's just one thing I'd like to know, Professor,' said Saul. 'Why are you going to all this trouble to help me?'

The Professor held the end of a long, slim cigar over the glass chimney of the kerosene lamp. When it had ignited properly, he said: 'Let's just say that I knew your father a long time ago.' He looked at Saul for a moment. 'I guess you're going to turn out very much like him. I hope you have the same speed with your body as he did.'

'Well, I ain't that bad with a gun,' admitted Saul. 'Course, with ammunition the price it is I ain't been able to practise much. But right since I can remember my Ma used to make me practise drawin'. First it was with a toy pistol, later with this Colt.' He pulled it from the holster and showed it to the Professor. 'That was my Dad's gun,' he said with a note of reverence in his voice.

The Professor regarded the gun for a moment.

'That was a good gun in its time,' he said. 'But I'm afraid if you've got any ideas of using that against Lew O'Hara and the rest you'd better forget them. There are faster guns now. Tomorrow we'll get you outfitted back in Juanita and then you're going to meet a man who can probably teach you more about firearms than anyone else in the West.'

Saul began to mutter his thanks, but the Professor just nodded his head and bid him good night.

As the youth climbed between the blankets he could hardly believe what was happening to him. For the first time he was away from Paradise and away from his mother and her endless talk about his father's killing. Now the days of talk were over. Soon he would be able to translate all those words into action, and it was all due to Professor Coffin. He felt he should be very grateful to him, this strange wandering newspaperman who obviously had once been a friend of his father. And yet there was a question mark in his mind, a vague unease, but this vanished as he was overtaken by sleep.

\* \* \*

The next day was one of sheer joy for Saul Powers. Soon after breakfast he and the Professor rode into Juanita and hitched their horses to the rail outside the shop of Reuben Jenkins, Gunsmith. Inside there was a bewildering array of new and second-hand guns. The wall was lined with rifles, including old Fogartys, brass-framed Henrys, Spencers, Springfield carbines, Robinson repeaters, heavy calibre Sharps and the popular Remingtons and Winchesters.

'Good morning, gents,' said Reuben Jenkins amiably from behind a glass-topped case of revolvers. 'What can I sell you this morning?'

'I want a six-gun and a rifle for this young man,' said the Professor. 'And we want the best. No old second-hand, worn out irons for us.'

'Well, you've come to the right place,' said Jenkins. 'I reckon I've got the best selection of hand guns and rifles in this State. Come over here, son, and look at this case. These are all new models. Now as you see, we have a very nice line in Smith and Wessons.'

Saul shook his head.

'I guess it's got to be a Colt,' he said, looking down at the various revolvers laying on a velvet cloth. One in the centre caught his eye. It was a Colt Frontier with a white bone handle. There was almost a hungry expression on his face as he looked at it. Never before had he seen such a beautiful gun. The Professor watched him coolly.

'You like that one, boy?'

'Yes, sirree,' said Saul, an eager smile on his bony face for once. 'I guess that's the prettiest gun I've ever seen.'

'It sure is a fancy one,' agreed Reuben Jenkins, 'an' it's beautifully balanced. Try it.'

'It feels pretty good all right,' said Saul, as he held it in his hand.

'Better try some others,' said the Professor.

'Certainly, gents, certainly/ said Reuben Jenkins. And for the next quarter of an hour a succession of guns passed through Saul's hands, but he kept returning to the bone-handled Frontier. There was something about this gun which told him it was meant to be his.

'I guess this is the one, Professor,' he said.

The Professor nodded his head in agreement.

'And now we'd better take a rifle.'

'Take a look at this, gents,' said Reuben Jenkins. 'It's the new model Marlin-Ballard. It's a mighty fine weapon. It takes a forty-five-seventy cartridge.' He demonstrated the lever action and then passed it over to Saul who hefted it, then handed it back.

'I guess it should be a Winchester,' he said. 'Then I won't have to carry two lots of ammunition.'

'I guess you're right there, sir,' said Reuben Jenkins. 'The best marriage the West has known was between the Colt Frontier and the Winchester Seventy-Three.'

A few minutes later Saul was the possessor of two new guns, a holster, a saddle sheath for the Winchester, and a large amount of .44-40 ammunition. As they returned to the tumbledown house a grizzled old man raised himself painfully from the steps on which he had been sitting. As the two riders dismounted he approached them, dragging his left leg.

'Howdy, Professor,' he said. 'I come like you asked in your letter. Is this the feller?' and he indicated Saul with a jerk of his head.

'That's right, Cole,' said the Professor. He turned to Saul. 'This is Cole Allard. A long time ago he was a gunsmith back East. Then he came West on the wagons and became one of the best shots north of the border.'

Cole Allard spat into the dust.

'That was all a long time ago,' he said. 'And it all finished when a damn Yankee bullet caught me at Bull Run. I'm all paralysed down one side now, and I ain't fit for anythin'. Sometimes I wish the guy who fired that bullet had been a bit more accurate.'

'Come and have a drink, old timer,' said the Professor tactfully. 'You're still the best man in the country for the job I want you to do. This here is the son of Luke Powers and I want you to teach him everything you know about guns so he'll be as formidable as his Dad. He's got some hard gun work ahead of him.'

Cole Allard nodded.

'Let's take a look at that Colt you've got there, boy,' he said. 'My, it's got a pretty fine handle but you'll soon learn that handles ain't everythin'. Now the first thing we'll have to do is a bit of filin' on the trigger spring, and we'll take a look at the holster, and see how much we have to cut away there. Then we'll get down to real practisin', and by that I don't mean just practisin' on the draw; you've got to learn to shoot fast and straight.

'There's one thing you must know from the start: it's better to shoot straight than fast. I guess you've heard tell of Wyatt Earp. He ain't nobody's fool and he told me once when he was deputy-marshal of Tombstone how he managed to survive so many battles and never even get scratched. He said: "The other feller usually fired first but being in such a hurry his first shot always missed. By the time he was ready to fire his second I had fired my first.

And I never missed, because I took my time." You always remember them words, boy. Now, Professor, you get out that bottle of rye, and we'll start makin' a real gun out of this dandy-lookin' Colt.'

And so the education of the young gunfighter began. Cole Allard was a hard master. He never praised, but heaped the most horrible oaths on Saul whenever he failed on the finest point. The old man would stand him in the square yard in front of the house in the hot sun while he sat on the verandah, a bottle of whisky within easy reach. At the far end was a row of scarecrows, each of which had been allotted a number. Saul would have to stand in the sun, sometimes for minutes on end, sometimes for half an hour. Suddenly the old man would yell, 'Number Five!' and the boy would whip out his Colt and send a bullet crashing in the direction of the dummy.

If the heat or the tension in not knowing when the order was coming next caused him to be slow in his reactions, the old man would curse and tell him he was a disgrace to his father's memory. When this phase was over, scarecrows were planted at different sides of the yard, so when Saul was given a number he sometimes had to spin round at the same time as drawing.

There was ordinary target practice every day, both with the Colt and the Winchester, and in this way many, many dollars' worth of ammunition was used up. Sometimes the Professor watched but even when Saul was perforating old bean cans which Cole Allard was flinging in the air he never commented.

One day, about two months after Saul had come to the old house outside Juanita, Cole Allard said to the Professor: 'Waal, there's your gunfighter, Professor. There is not another thing I can teach him. With what he's learned here, coupled with his old man's reflexes, I guess you've got yourself the deadliest hombre the West has seen for a mighty long time. I just hope you'll know what to do with him.'

    The Professor nodded.

    'Come over here, boy,' he called.

    Saul, who had been blazing away at a cleverly constructed moving target which involved the sails of a windmill, walked across the sunlit yard to the gloom of the verandah.

    'School's over now,' the Professor announced. 'Tomorrow we're starting on the trail to Gila Springs. We've got an appointment there with Lew O'Hara, but he doesn't know a thing about it yet.'

# CHAPTER 3

There was a carnival atmosphere in Gila Springs, flags flew in a lazy wind and bunting was displayed on the false fronts of the ugly buildings on Silver Street. In Big Lew O'Hara's Lucky Lode saloon the miners were killing their thirst with their usual enthusiasm while the other side of the town, the respectable side, citizens promenaded decorously in sombre Sunday best along the wooden sidewalks.

For once the womenfolk of the sober citizens did not cluck their tongues when they passed the Lucky Lode, and for once the girls who danced there did not put their tongues out at them. At last the little town had a feeling of unity and tolerance, thanks to Big Lew.

From an upper window of the saloon he surveyed the festive scene with satisfaction. He was a big, smooth, swarthy man, dressed in a perfectly fitting dove-grey morning coat and a white cravat complete with a diamond pin which flashed expensively in the noon sun.

Down the street a band struck up on a specially erected platform and couples formed up to dance to the lively music.

'It sure is a great day – my day,' said Lew, lighting a fat cigar. 'Damme, if it ain't the smartest thing I ever done.'

'Lordy sakes, but we are havin' a love affair with ourselves this fine day,' came a feminine voice behind him.

'You cut that out, Topaz – an' drop that

goshdarned phoney Southern accent,' growled Big Lew.

'You just be quiet, Mistah O'Hara. Ah'll have yew know mah Daddy was a Southern gentleman before them damn Yankees came an' burned our mansion an' stole our land. It broke mah Daddy's heart – an' that's the reason Ah'm workin' for a cotton-pickin' son of a bitch like yew.'

'Nice words from a Southern gentlewoman,' grinned Big Lew, turning to see the curvaceous form of Topaz reclining in a rather brief but profusely feathered costume on his bed.

'Now, I suggest you go down stairs an' offer some of our customers your famous Southern hospitality. I don't pay you good dollars to lay about here an' be sassy.'

'So what do you pay me good dollars for, Mistah O'Hara?' asked Topaz, sitting up and giving Big Lew a shrewd look. 'Or ain't you so interested since you met that mousy little school-marm?'

'Shut up, Topaz, it ain't your business.'

'Ain't it just,' said Topaz, her accent slipping for an instant. 'Waal, that's where you're goddam wrong...Lordy, lordy, Mistah O'Hara. Ah've helped yew all build up this saloon from a cabin that our slaves would have walked out of in disgust. An, now, just 'cause yew've met a little no-account schoolmarm yew have gone coon crazy, buildin' a school an' all. Do yew hope someday there'll be your statue in Silver Street...do yew want to be respectable all of a sudden, Mistah O'Hara?'

'Don't be a fool, and fer Gawd's sake stop callin' me "Mistah O'Hara" – you ain't in the Old Colonial Home now, an' you never were. You know as well as I do why I've built that school. Times are changin' here. A few years back it was a rip-roarin' minin' town an' if a man was big enough he stayed on top. Now that's changin'. Tradesmen an' sod-busters have come – law-abidin',

Gawd-fearin' people. Why there's even a hot gospel hall now. An' all the time the wives are becomin' more powerful. At first we just laughed at their petitions to close us down, but now it ain't so funny,. Once this was a real man's town, but it won't be much longer.

'So I'm smart. I build the citizens a school, I get them a teacher from the East an' I pay for everythin'. That is our insurance to stay open. They won't worry about the profit on the Demon Drink when it's educatin' their kids. This way I'll still be King of Gila.'

'We all should have moved on,' retorted Topaz. 'There's plenty of frontier towns left. There's new ones openin' up further west, maybe we could have started a real high-class establishment in Tombstone... The trouble is, Mistah O'Hara, yew are gettin' tired an' fat.'

'Don't call me...Never mind, think what you like, an' if you don't like it vamoose back to dear old Dixie an' may you rot there.'

He stalked out, briefly angry and tired of Topaz, though he had to admit she had her uses. One of them was that she packed in the customers, and if only she would keep her mouth shut she was a miner's dream of heaven.

In the street his good humour returned. Someone cried 'Hurrah for Big Lew' and people – respectable people – smiled at him. A few weeks ago they would have turned their faces away.

'Everyone has their price,' thought Big Lew philosophically.

'Reckon we're ready if you are,' said the town constable coming up.

'Let's get on with the show,' Big Lew replied.

The band struck up a march, a procession formed magically and the customers flowed out of the Lucky Lode, some clutched bottles so that thirst would not be one of the dangers they would have to face. With Big Lew, the local bank manager and the New Jerusalem

Meeting Hall padre at its head, the procession flowed down Silver Street to where a pleasant new timber schoolhouse stood on the outskirts of town.

Using the porch as a platform the bank manager, who was also President of the Gila Springs Improvement Association, gave a long speech thanking their fellow citizen, Mister Lewis O'Hara, for the new school which was a sure sign that prosperity was coming to the town, which was also reflected in the recent establishment of his bank...

The padre, on the other hand, kept his contribution short. He was in best form when calling down hellfire on drunkards, but under the circumstances he thought such sentiments would not be appropriate. He muttered a few platitudes about the different factions of the town coming together to form a single community.

'Amen, amen,' responded his flock.

'Hallelujah!' yelled the patrons of the Lucky Lode, discharging their firearms above their heads in enthusiasm.

'I only aim to do one thing up here,' said Big Lew when it was his turn. 'An' that is to introduce you to Miss Melinda Blackwell who is going to be the teacher at my school. Miss Melinda, come up here and meet the folk of Gila Springs.'

Blushing prettily, a fair-haired girl in pale blue joined him on the platform.

'Oh, thank you, Lewis,' she whispered, looking up at him with adoration in her clear grey eyes.

'Folks,' began Big Lew, 'once Gila Springs was a bad town, the Bowie and the Colt were boss and it weren't no place for a lady. But it's all a-changin' ...we are growin' up, especially now that education has come at last in the pretty shape of Miss Melinda...'

Prolonged cheers, while the sight of the young teacher caused quite a few dollars worth of ammunition to be discharged skywards.

'Now, it's a holiday, so let's spend it the best we can.'

The band struck up and there were more cheers and clapping and cries of 'Long live Big Lew!' Suddenly he realised that they were cheering him, that overnight he had become a hero.

With pride he looked at the sea of faces before him, yelling faces, laughing faces, happy faces...Only one struck him with a slight uneasy sensation he could not analyse. It was as though it briefly touched a long forgotten chord of memory, yet it was a feeling rather than anything concrete. A moment later it was dismissed as Big Lew turned to Melinda Blackwell. But the youth in the front row with the burning blue eyes continued to watch the King of Gila Springs with a strangely expressionless stare.

\* \* \*

Melinda Blackwell sat at her new desk in her new classroom. Big Lew leaned against the far wall, a fat cigar champed between his teeth.

'I think that what you have done is the most wonderful thing I have heard of,' she said. 'Since I've been here I've heard people speak of you – well – unkindly. I guess they don't like your saloon...'

'Yeah, that's the way the people you mix with think about me,' said Big Lew. 'On the other side of Silver Street I'm not such a bad fella. The men at the diggin's have a mean, hard life. I give 'em a good time, a little taste of high livin', a chance to have them a few hours of fun. I guess that ain't such a bad thing.'

'Yes, but the gambling – and the drink...'

'The respectable folk of this town have their women an' families. The way they live they may as well be back East, only it ain't so comfortable. My customers are lonely men livin' in sod huts. They're different, the only place they've got is my saloon.'

'I can see that, and I do think a lot of the people who criticised the Lucky Lode are narrow minded, even hypocritical. They cheered you today after you'd given them something. But what shocked me was that shooting last week. I hear that one man shot down another in cold blood in your place.'

Big Lew shrugged. 'This is still a violent land full of violent men,' he explained. 'I don't expect you to understand it, but death becomes pretty commonplace on the frontier. What you have to do is bring up the kids so they're a different breed...'

'I shall certainly try,' she answered. 'But tell me one thing, Lewis...have you ever killed a man?'

'Not just a man, men,' he answered simply. 'By your standards, Miss Blackwell. I've led a bad life. There are many things I would prefer to forget...Once I was a member of a desperate gang. It seems a long time ago.'

Melinda was now standing in front of him, her eyes shining, her fingers lightly on his chest, 'Then, Lewis,' she said, her voice soft with emotion, 'I admire you more than ever. Despite your past, you have a faith, a wonderful faith in the future, in the children of this town...'

Suddenly she felt his arms tighten about her, she looked up at his strong, suave face and closed her eyes. But the expected kiss never came. Instead a voice cut through the classroom: 'Hogwash! Miss Blackwell, if yew will believe that little ole line of talk Mistah O'Hara has been handin' out, yew are even more stupid than Ah believed it possible for a no-account piece of Yankee trash to be...'

Melinda spun round, to see Topaz standing in the doorway, a startling figure in her Lucky Lode finery.

'Who...' she began.

'Get outa here,' snapped Big Lew.

'Lordy me, it's "Get outa here," is it, Mistah O'Hara. Now, if Ah don't recollect wrong them weren't the words yew used to me last night.'

Melinda flushed crimson.

'Please leave my classroom, Miss...'

'Topaz,' came the reply in an over-sweet voice. 'Sure, Ah'll leave, but Ah think your friend Mistah O'Hara had better come too. There's a fight broken out over a game of faro...'

'Goddam it, why didn't you say so before,' cried Big Lew. He ran from the room, his hand straying to the gun he always wore under his frock coat.

'Now, Missy Blackwell, keep your cotton-pickin' little fingers off man man. You ain't in his class. An' just get it into your pretty little ole head that the only reason Mistah O'Hara built this school an' brought you all the way from the East was so he could insure himself against the closing of the Lucky Lode. Don't you think he's the clever one? An' remember – as one lady to another – if you make sweet talk at him again, Ah'll scratch out your goddam eyes.'

Alone, Melinda burst into tears. The day had started so well, and now it was ruined. She did not know what to think anymore. Suddenly there was a knock at the door.

'Come in,' she called, gulping back her sobs and hastily wiping her eyes on a wisp of a handkerchief.

A thin, white-haired youth walked in. She noticed with distaste that a bone-handled revolver hung low on his hip. He looked so young to be carrying an instrument of death.

'Pardon me, ma'am,' said Saul. 'I had a message for Mister O'Hara.'

'He – he's gone back to his – his saloon,' said Melinda.

'Why, ma'am, is there somethin' wrong?'

'No, nothing, thank you. I was a bit overcome by the excitement.'

'I guess it has been an excitin' time. A school of your own, an' you so young.' For a moment she almost smiled. He was younger than she. Then she frowned.

There was something about the young man that made her feel uneasy. He was so slim, and yet it was not a thinness caused by hunger. Although he hardly moved when he was talking there was a deep restlessness about him, and when he looked at her with his surprisingly blue eyes she felt suddenly unsure of herself.

'You said you had a message?'

'Yes, ma'am. Mind if I put it on the blackboard. Then he'll see it when he comes back. There ain't no hurry, this piece of business has waited for some years.'

Saul picked up a piece of chalk and wrote in a childish print Numbers 35, 19.

'I guess my hand writin' ain't much,' said Saul, 'but my Ma sure used to scripture me. Goodbye, ma'am.'

He was gone. Melinda walked over to the blackboard and looked at the chalked writing, then, out of a drawer in her desk she took a Bible. She turned to Numbers, found the chapter and verse and to her horror read: *The revenger of blood himself shall slay the murderer: when he meeteth him, he shall slay him.*

\* \* \*

In a sleazy rooming house in one of the alleys that ran off Silver Street, Saul Powers sat on his bed cleaning the Colt Frontier in the dismal light of an oil lamp. On the opposite bed lay the long form of the Professor, one of his slim cigars pointing upwards at the dingy ceiling.

'How do you feel now you've seen him?' he asked.

'Sort of strange,' said Saul. 'I guess, to be honest, Professor, I feel a bit scared. Scared of messing it up, maybe.'

'What else do you feel?' asked the Professor. 'Hate?'

'Yeah, I feel hate all right. It was pretty durned strange standing there lookin' at a man I knew had emptied his gun into my father. I wish we could get on with it. I don't like this hangin' around. I could have gunned him down today.'

'It's got to be set up properly,' said the Professor. 'You've got to take him in a fair fight. For one thing right now he's a pretty popular man in this town. If there was any suspicion that you'd murdered him you'd finish up doing a jig at the end of a lariat. The other thing is it's got to be done so you start to build a reputation as a gunfighter,'

'I ain't worried about any reputation,' said Saul. 'I just want to get on with the work I know I've got to do.'

'Sure, sure,' said the Professor soothingly. 'But what you don't realise is the help a reputation as a fast gun will be to you. Believe me, son, it's half the battle. When you stand face to face with some other guy, if he knows he's up against a top gun his nerve is likely to crack. There's more to this business than just pulling out a gun and letting fly.'

'I guess you're right,' Saul admitted.

'Sure I am,' said the Professor. 'And the other thing is don't go forgetting what Cole told you. When it comes to the showdown between you and Lew O'Hara, shoot him in the belly. It may not kill him outright but it'll put him down and you can finish him off with a second shot. The only man I ever heard of who could win every time by shooting his enemies in the head was Hickok, and with the greatest respect, son, I don't think you're in his class yet.'

Saul grinned. 'Maybe not yet, Professor, but some day I will. Now then, what's the next move?'

'I think we'll seize the advantage as it comes up,' he replied. 'Leave it to me, boy, I'll make sure that it's done properly. You'd better get some sleep now. I want you in top condition when the time comes.'

'Okay.' Saul kicked off his boots, wriggled out of his Levis and his worn shirt, and slipped under the blankets, having first placed the Frontier beneath his pillow. Within a minute he was asleep, his face strangely relaxed and innocent.

\* \* \*

The spirit of celebration at Gila Springs continued long after sundown. In the New Jerusalem Gospel Hall the worthy element of the town performed decorous formation dances to the music of a fiddle band. In the Lucky Lode there was dancing of another sort. To the cheers of the miners a number of young ladies gave their version of the Can-Can on the low stage at the far end of the saloon.

Big Lew stood at his accustomed place by the bar. A glass of champagne, his favourite drink, was within easy reach. His eyes wandered over the lively scene with satisfaction.

'I guess this is one of the busiest nights we've had/ he said to Topaz as she passed him, a frosty look on her otherwise sensuous face. 'A night like this could just about pay for the school,' he continued. 'Why, durn me, it's almost worth buildin' schools to get the custom goin' like this.'

'Ah don't find your conversation at all interestin' tonight,' said Topaz, and she minced away from him. A moment later there was a roll on the drum and the leader of Lucky Lode's small band of musicians stood up.

'Gentlemen,' he called above the din of the

roistering miners, 'for your entertainment Miss Topaz, that beautiful belle from South Carolina, will perform that classic biblical entertainment, the Dance of the Seven Veils.'

The cheers were deafening. The velvet curtain was drawn back and Topaz began her exotic number. Several of the veils had floated to the floor of the stage when Big Lew heard the saloon doors creak behind him. He turned to see Melinda Blackwell enter and stand dazed by the sudden glare of light and the colourful spectacle of the saloon. She looked around wildly. Luckily for her the patrons were too engrossed in Topaz's celebrated dance to look her way, otherwise she would have been subjected to an embarrassing welcome. Her eyes caught sight of Big Lew and, with a look of relief, she hurried over to the bar.

'Lewis,' she said, 'I've got to talk to you.'

'What is it, my dear?' he asked.

'Something strange happened at the schoolhouse just after you'd gone. A boy came, said he had a message for you and he wrote something on the blackboard.' Hurriedly, she told Big Lew how she had looked up the verse in the Bible.

'I had to come and warn you,' she added, 'I feel you are in danger.'

'It just sounds kinda silly to me,' mused Big Lew. 'I guess I have made enemies in the past, but if they were goin' to do anythin' about it they'd probably shoot me in the back. They certainly wouldn't go writin' messages on a blackboard.'

He noticed the look of distaste on her face.

'Anyway, this ain't no place for a lady like you. Come on, and I'll walk you back to your room. I must say I sure appreciate the fact that you came here to warn me.'

At that moment a cheer rose from the miners. On the stage Topaz had shed her final veil and stood in a brief spangled costume and provocative black stockings. For a moment she acknowledged the applause and then her eye caught sight of Melinda. Without a word she ran down from the stage and fought her way through the press of miners, slipping neatly past the arms that tried to embrace her.

'I warned you!' she hissed when she got close to the schoolteacher. Diving forward, she began to pull the girl's hair with one hand, slapping her about the face with the other. Next moment the two girls were rolling on the floor and, to the surprise of the delighted onlookers, the schoolteacher seemed to be giving as good as she got. Her hand clawed the dancer's cheek leaving bloody furrows.

Topaz gave a scream of pain and tried to get her fingers round her adversary's neck, but she only succeeded in tearing her dress. Over and over they rolled, scratching and biting like two jungle animals.

Big Lew watched calmly, a smug smile on his face, for he knew perfectly well that the fight was over him. It had flattered his vanity. What did surprise him was that the quiet little schoolteacher, whom Topaz described as a mouse, was getting the upper hand. Suddenly she was kneeling on her opponent. Grabbing a handful of the saloon girl's hair, she lifted her head and then smashed it down on the floor with such force that Topaz was stunned. She shuddered and her grip on the girl from the East relaxed. Slowly the schoolteacher got to her feet. Her dress was in tatters. In vain she tried to hold her ripped blouse modestly across her breast while a thin trickle of blood ran down the side of her face. In her grey eyes there was a strange look of triumph.

'I'll bid you goodnight now,' she said to Big Lew between her gasps. 'Please remember my warning and tell your girl friend when she wakes up that if she tries any tricks again she'll know what to expect.'

Then, with considerable dignity, she walked towards the door, leaving an awed silence behind her. On the floor the spread-eagled Topaz gave a moan. Big Lew callously picked up a jug of cold water and threw it on her face. Her eyes opened and she struggled into a sitting position. Big Lew gave a signal to the band. Music struck up and the customers switched their gaze once more to the stage.

'That goddam hellcat,' Topaz spat. 'I'll get her for this if I have to swing for it.'

'Go and clean yourself up, you look disgustin',' said Big Lew. He drained his champagne and muttered: 'Goddam women!'

With this undignified fight he felt his whole day had gone sour on him. He was also vaguely troubled over the warning that Melinda had come to give him. One thing he was sure about. Topaz must go. She wasn't the only girl in the West, who could do the Dance of the Seven Veils, and anyway, Miss Melinda Blackwell would probably approve.

Pleased at the prospect of bearing bad news, he stalked off in the direction of Topaz's dressing room.

* * *

Saul Powers stood in the centre of his mean bedroom, the bone-handled Colt Frontier strapped low down on his thigh. He stood on the balls of his feet, his arms relaxed, his hands swinging free. From his bed the Professor regarded the young man through his blue tinted spectacles. Suddenly he clapped his hands. At this signal Saul's right hand grasped the butt of the revolver and in a blur of movement he had raised it to eye level. He was going through his regular daily practice so essential to the successful gunfighter.

'Not bad,' commented the Professor. 'Get your left leg farther forward. If your feet are too close together you haven't got such a firm stand.'

Saul   nodded   and   bolstered   his   weapon.

Immediately the Professor clapped his hands again and once more the Frontier appeared like magic.

'That will do for this morning, boy.'

Saul sat down on his bed and began replacing the cartridges in the chambers.

'When am I going to get down to cases with Lew O' Hara?' he asked.

'I guess the showdown should be tomorrow,' said the Professor. 'Now this is what I want you to do. Get over to the Lucky Lode this afternoon and call him out. Don't wear your gun.'

'Why the hell not?' asked Saul in surprise.

'I want this to be done the proper way,' explained the Professor. 'If you carry your gun he's likely to draw on you on the spot – and who knows how it would go with a man like him. One of his men may get you from behind. If it's fought out in Silver Street it'll be fair and square and there won't be any chance of you having to stand a murder charge afterwards. Yesterday Lew O'Hara was the most popular man in town, even with the respectable folk. But now they've changed their minds a bit, I guess.'

'How so?'

'Last night O'Hara's mistress attacked the new schoolmarm, and the two girls had a rough and tumble on the saloon floor. Funnily enough, the schoolmarm didn't come off so bad. But even so the women of the town are saying that the Lucky Lode ought to be closed down if that sort of thing is going to happen. After all, they've got their school now and gratitude doesn't last very long. So as I said, if you're seen to shoot O'Hara down fair and square there is not the danger of a murder charge or a lynching.'

'Okay, it sounds sense to me,' said Saul. 'I'll be glad when it's over. Tell me one thing, Professor.'

'Yes?'

'Have you ever killed a man?'

The Professor smiled and shook his head. 'The pen is mightier than the sword – and the Colt,' he said. 'I've no need to carry weapons.'

'I wonder what it feels like,' Saul mused. 'It must be a mighty strange feelin'. At least if you haven't killed anybody I guess you've seen plenty of shootings, havin' known Frankie Kelso and guys like that.'

'Yes, I've seen plenty,' said the Professor. 'You get pretty used to it. I think after the first time you won't give it another thought. It isn't all that special.'

'I'll give you another thought all right,' said Saul. 'I'm gonna enjoy it too much for that. They say revenge is sweet and I guess it'll be the sweetest thing I'll ever know. Now I think I'll go down and get me some air.'

He went down the stairs and sat on a packing case outside the rooming house. It was Sunday morning and the town, after the celebration the day before, had an air of hangover about it. The only movement was a small group of sober citizens walking in the direction of the Gospel Hall for a Sunday prayer meeting.

Saul leaned back, his eyes narrowed in the glare of the sunlight. Tomorrow he would be face to face with the first of his father's killers. In his head rang the promise he had made to his mother, the promise he had made every day through childhood. He knew that nothing else mattered except to exterminate those five evil men. The Professor had talked about him gaining a reputation as a gunfighter. He didn't care about this. Nor did he have any idea what he would do when his trail of vengeance was over. That was in the future and the future was a long way off.

In his mind he saw the picture of the murder again – of his father's jerking body, and the five men sitting on their horses calmly firing at him. He remembered Big Lew O'Hara. He had been thinner then, but his face and his black moustache were still the same, etched in Saul's memory. Maybe he had built the town a school, maybe he was going respectable, but he had shown no mercy that hot morning twelve years ago and Saul would show him none now.

A young woman came along the sidewalk. She wore a dark grey gown and bonnet and her prayer book in her hand showed that she was on her way to the gospel meeting. When she saw Saul she stopped.

'I looked up that verse in the Bible,' she said abruptly. 'It was a terrible verse.'

'Yes, ma'am,' said Saul, 'I guess it was.'

'Are you going to try and kill Mister O'Hara?'

'Yes, ma'am,' said Saul, his voice flat and expressionless.

'But why?' she asked angrily. 'What can he have done to you to make you ready to stain your hands with blood at your age?'

'I guess it ain't any of your business, ma'am. It's somethin' that happened a long time ago. Maybe O'Hara doesn't even remember it very clearly any more. But I do. Not a day has passed when I've not seen it happen in my mind.'

'But whatever it was, two wrongs don't make a right,' the girl said. 'He's not the same man he was years ago. Whatever he was then – and I can imagine he led a wild life from what he told me – he's a different man now. He's had a brutal life perhaps, but now he's changing. Why, he built the school and brought me all the way out from the East to teach the children of this town. That is not the action of a bad man. Please, I beg of you, go away. Nothing you can do now can alter the past. Go while you're still alive, for I think you would stand little chance against a man like Lewis O'Hara.'

'I figure that remains to be seen,' said Saul. 'But

you'll excuse me saying so, ma'am, but when it comes to violence, from what I hear tell, you don't exactly turn the other cheek yourself.'

The girl flushed crimson. 'I was attacked – it was in self-defence. I didn't go looking for trouble.'

Saul shrugged. 'If it gives you any consolation, ma'am, it'll be a fair fight,' he said. 'I'm going to give him more chance than he gave my – '

'I can see there's nothing more I can say to you,' snapped Melinda. 'You're an arrogant young fool. You seem to be in love with death. Perhaps you think you're a second Billy the Kid.'

Again Saul shrugged. 'Miss Blackwell,' he said, 'just let me give you one word of advice. You may know a lot about bein' a schoolmarm, but you don't savvy how things are in the West. My advice to you is to go back to the world you know and understand.'

'You won't get rid of me that easy,' she retorted. 'Some way or other I'm going to stop you, and maybe some day you'll live to thank me for it.'

With that she hurried away. Saul watched her go with a curious expression on his face. He realised that for the first time in his life he had been talking to a very attractive young woman. It was a shame their attitudes were so different.

Then his lips clamped together in a grim line. The very last thing a man could do with his destiny would be to allow himself to think of girls! It was all right for other fellows, who had nothing ahead of them to accomplish except getting married sometime and settling down. But he had a full-time job of killing ahead of him, and he remembered how Cole Allard had told him that he must be dedicated to his gun as a great musician is to his instrument – or a priest to his calling. Perhaps the latter was the best example. He knew that he must be dedicated to the Colt alone.

* * *

It was early in the afternoon when Saul pushed his way through the doors of the Lucky Lode and walked towards the baize-covered table where Big Lew O'Hara was amusing himself with a game of solitaire. So far there were very few customers and the old roustabout was still sprinkling fresh sawdust on the floor.

'Hello, youngster,' said Big Lew. 'Come for a drink or a game?'

'Neither,' said Saul. 'Tve come to call you out.' There was a long silence, then Big Lew rose to his feet, his hand held close to his gun belt.

'You ain't wearin' a gun, kid,' he said. 'Is this some sort of a joke?'

'I'll be wearin' a gun when I meet you in Silver Street tomorrow. That's if you have the guts to come out an' face me,' replied Saul.

Big Lew's eyes narrowed. 'Ain't I seen you somewheres before?'

'Maybe,' said Saul. 'But I guess you were too busy killing my father to notice me playin' on the verandah.'

'My Gawd! Luke Powers! You must be Luke's boy.'

'Right in one, an' I'm calling you out, mister.'

'Look, kid, I ain't afraid of you, but I don't want to have to kill you as well. What happened twelve years ago is old history now. I ain't a-goin' to meet you.'

'You're a goddammed coward,' shouted Saul. At his words the few people in the saloon looked around in time to see him pick up a glass of whisky from a nearby table and fling it into Big Lew's face.

'...an' a goddam liar!'

'You've asked for it,' snarled Big Lew, the whisky trickling down his face which had become an angry red. 'I'll be on Silver Street tomorrow mornin'.'

"'Bout nine o'clock?" suggested Saul.

Big Lew nodded and began to wipe his face with a black silk handkerchief. His hand was trembling with rage at the insult – the worst that a man could be given in the West.

Without a word, Saul turned on his heel and walked out of the Lucky Lode.

# CHAPTER 4

'All right, you fellas, open your eyes and put your hands where I can see 'em!'

The command echoed in Saul's mind through layers of sleep. Next instant he was fully awake, though his eyelids had not shown a flicker. Imperceptibly, his hand began to move under the blankets to where the Colt Frontier made a hard lump beneath his straw filled pillow.

'Wake up, I say!' came the voice harshly. Something hard was pressing against Saul's chest – the cold barrel of a gun. Under this threat Saul sat up. In the dim light of a lantern he could see two men, each armed with a scatter gun. On the opposite bed the Professor was already sitting up, his hands level with his shoulders.

'Did Big Lew send you along to fight his battle for him?' he demanded in a thick voice.

'I'm the town constable,' came the reply. 'I've come to take you both in.'

'On what charge?' the Professor demanded.

'There ain't no charge. It's what they call "protective custody." My job is to stop murder, an' if this kid meets Big Lew tomorrow, that's jest what it'd be.'

'Who are you savin' – him or me?' asked Saul.

The constable ignored him.

'Keep 'em covered, Jeb,' he told his companion. Deftly he found Saul's gun.

'Get your clothes on, fellas,' he said. 'You're spendin' the night in the jail-house. Tomorrow you'll be put on the stage outa here. An' don't cuss like that, boy. If your Ma knew what I was a-doin' she'd be plumb thankful.'

Saul gave a bitter snort of laughter.

'That goes to show you ain't acquainted with my Ma,' he said. 'Say, mister, who put you up to this? It wouldn't happen to be that new schoolmarm, would it?'

'Forget the questions, jest get your clothes on.'

Slowly the two men pulled on their garments while the constable and his mate kept them covered. Then they were marched down the moonlit street to the small building that served as the constable's office and local jail.

Inside they found it to be a single room, divided by iron bars. The two companions were locked on one side while Jeb settled down behind the rough desk on the other.

'Big Lew ain't gonna thank you,' Saul said as he threw himself on one of the plank bunks that was attached to the wall by a chain. 'The story'll get around that he had you do this because he was yeller.'

'Save your breath,' the constable replied. 'An' don't get no fancy ideas about bustin' out. No one's ever got outa here alive, ain't that so, Jeb?'

Jeb nodded and settled his big boots on the desk. Out of a cupboard the constable took a bottle of whisky.

'This'll keep the cold out,' he told Jeb. 'If the boys behave give 'em a dose of Red Eye – if they don't give 'em a dose of buckshot.'

Jeb grinned at the witticism.

'I'll be back to put 'em on the stage,' said the constable. 'Goodnight, fellas.'

'Fry in hell,' muttered Saul.

The Professor lay down on the other bunk, pulled the blanket over himself and prepared to go to sleep.

'Can't you do somethin'?' Saul demanded.

'Not right now, boy. There isn't any sense in getting all riled up when the drop's on you.'

'That's the way to take it,' agreed Jeb. 'You boys behave yourselves an' I'll give you a good breakfast in the mornin'. How's that for a deal?'

Saul turned his face to the wall, white with anger. To have come so close to his enemy only to lose the chance of vengeance at the last moment almost brought tears to his eyes. What a fool he had been to go to sleep so calmly before the day of reckoning! He felt physically sick at the thought of being hustled out of town like some unwanted bum. And what added to his suppressed fury was the gentle snoring of the Professor. Now the chips were down it seemed that even he didn't care.

'Have a drink, son,' said Jeb coming over to the bars and proffering a glass of whisky. 'It gets pretty cold here at night.'

Saul shook his head.

'Guess you feel pretty sore about this,' said Jeb sympathetically. 'That's jest because you're young. I once saw Big Lew blast down a man. It was a fair fight, but this fella jest hadn't a chance in hell. You may not fancy what's happened, but at least you'll stay alive.'

'Spare me the sermon,' retorted Saul. 'You're startin' to sound like that interferin' schoolmarm.'

Jeb laughed, drained the whisky and went back to his seat. Soon his head began to nod, then it sank forward in sleep.

It jerked upright again when the door opened and a voice said: 'Just raise your little ole hands, mistah, an' no trouble will come to yew.'

Saul sat up on his bunk to see the figure of a girl in the lamplight. She wore a dark cloak and in her hand was a Williamson derringer. Jeb, still half asleep, looked at her stupidly.

'Don't get no notions about reachin' for that shot gun,' Topaz continued. 'If yew tried Ah'd have a bullet between your eyes quicker'n a snake can blink.'

'I'll take your word for it, ma'am,' said Jeb with a resigned shrug.

'That's fine an' dandy. Now, just unlock those pore gen'l'men an' we-all will be on our way.'

Jeb drew a key from his pocket and shambled over to the door of the cell. Saul ran out and took his gun from the drawer where the constable had placed it.

'Now get inside,' he ordered. Obediently Jeb entered the cell. 'Can I have my bottle of rye,' he said plaintively. 'I reckon it's gonna be a lonely night.'

Saul passed it through the bars to him while the Professor turned the key in the big lock.

'Gosh, ma'am, I don't know why you've taken this trouble, but I sure 'preciate it,' said Saul when they were outside.

'Ah'll tell yew why Ah did it,' Topaz replied in a bitter voice. 'That god-dammed O'Hara threw me out like Ah was some piece of no-account trash. Now Ah just hope yew settle my account when you settle your own.'

Saul nodded with understanding.

'Guess we'd better keep outa the way until tomorrow mornin',' he said.

'There's a lil ole miner's cabin 'bout a mile down the trail,' said Topaz. 'It's been empty for a year or more, you-all should be safe there. Ah'll be happy to show you gentlemen the way.'

The dust trail was like a white ribbon in the moonlight as the trio plodded away from Gila Springs. In the distance a coyote howled dismally, and further away another answered it.

Topaz and the Professor walked ahead. Saul heard the Professor say: 'As I'm a newspaperman, Miss Topaz, I wonder if you could give me a few details about yourself for our readers...'

'Oh surely,' Topaz replied. 'Mah Daddy – the Colonel everyone called him – had one of the biggest plantations south of the Mason-Dixon. Why, Ah remember like it was yesterday the balls that we used to have in the ole mansion, an' the dresses mah Mammy used to wear straight from Paris...'

# CHAPTER 5

The sun rose like a great disc of molten gold. For a few minutes it made the desert beautiful. In the eastern sky tatters of cloud became a flock of pink celestial sheep, while on the empty plain saguaros cast long grotesque shadows as they faced the new day. Soon the heat would come and the landscape, now crystal clear, would shimmer like a mirage in the tortured air; the rays of the new sun would burn the tin roofs of Gila Springs, awakening its citizens, whose faces had already begun to run with sweat. And when they opened their eyes they sensed this day was going to be different. They knew they were to see a duel to the death this morning on dusty Silver Street. Perhaps the Ancient Roman citizens jostling into the Coliseum experienced the same feeling of anticipation.

Leaving the Professor to make his I own way to the town, Saul circled the outskirts until he reached the old clapboard rooming house. Without disturbing the deaf woman who owned the place, he went up the stairs to his room. If he was going to meet Big Lew O'Hara in a gun duel he needed a holster for his bone-handled Colt. He laid it on his bed and was just buckling on the heavy gun belt when the door opened. He was about to make a dive for his weapon when he saw the barrel of a Remington single shot pistol. Behind this gun stood Melinda Blackwell, a determined look in her eye.

'Stay exactly where you are,' she ordered. 'I don't want to hurt you, but I'll do so if necessary. And remember, even though I come from the East I was raised on a farm and I was pretty fair at handling a gun.'

'I'll take your word on that,' said Saul. 'I suppose you've come to try an' stop me...'

That's right,' interjected the girl. 'I sensed there was something amiss when I woke this morning. I went down to the jail and found the guard locked in his cell. I had a hunch that you might come back here and – well – here I am. And here I'm going to stay until the stage leaves Gila Springs with you aboard.'

'And supposin' I don't want to go?'

'In that case I'll have to shoot you,' Melinda replied seriously. 'I won't shoot to kill you, but I'll put a bullet through your right arm. That'd stop any ideas of gunplay for a while.'

'You know,' Saul said quietly, 'for a schoolmarm you're a most surprising young woman. It's just a pity you're meddlin' with things you don't savvy.'

She smiled slightly. 'Comin' from you, I guess that's a compliment.'

'D'you mind if I sit down,' Saul asked. 'I feel rather silly standin' in the middle of the floor.'

'Certainly, but don't get too near that gun of yours.'

'Don't you worry about that. Even if I could get it I wouldn't use it on a lady.'

He sat down on the Professor's bed, quite relaxed. 'After a while my friend will be along,' he said. 'You won't be able to shoot both of us.'

'Who is that man – the Professor?' Melinda asked. There is something about him that makes me uneasy. Perhaps it's those blue glasses he wears.'

'He's the only man who's ever done me a kindness,' said Saul shortly. 'He used to be a friend of my father's long, long ago.'

Minutes passed. Saul said nothing, but he could

see that the waiting was starting to take effect on Melinda. Several times she licked her lips nervously, but the Remington stayed as firm as a rock.

'Just let me give you a word of advice,' said Saul at last. 'Even if you're holdin' somebody up with a gun, you've got to relax. Otherwise you'll get so tense that you're likely to pull the trigger just because your nerves are jumpy. I'd sure hate that to happen. You're much too pretty to be a murderess.'

'Better you than Lewis O'Hara,' Melinda retorted. 'At least he tries to do something for the community, whereas your ambition seems to become a petty little gunslinger.'

'I guess you must be kind of sweet on him,' said Saul. 'An' you're afraid for him. Funny thing is that when the town constable arrested me last night he said he was afraid for me. It will be interestin' to see who does win.'

'That's something you'll never know,' said Melinda.

'Won't I?' said Saul, and suddenly shifted his gaze to the door behind her.

'Hullo, Professor,' he cried. 'You're just in time!'

For a moment Melinda fell for the ruse. She turned her head slightly and her eyes flicked to the empty doorway. In a split second Saul was on his feet, diving across the room towards her. As her eyes returned to him she pulled the trigger. The heavy .50 slug cut an agonising groove through the muscles of Saul's upper arm. It was as though a white hot poker had been pressed against it. The pain made him dizzy and he collapsed back on the bed. Blood was flowing down his arm and dripping from the ends of his fingers.

'My God,' cried Melinda. 'What have I done?'

'You've ruined my arm, you bitch,' he gritted from between clenched teeth.

She threw down the smoking Remington, and, lifting her skirt, tore off a long strip from her petticoat. 'Let me bind it up,' she begged. 'I don't want you to bleed to death.'

'I can look after myself,' retorted Saul furiously. 'Just get outa my room before I forget you're a lady.'

'I can't leave you with that wound,' she said.

Saul looked at his bloody hand. He tried to open and close his fingers, but already they were stiffening up.

'If you want to be of some help go and get a doctor then,' he snapped. 'It feels like I'm losin' the use of my hand.'

'I must stop the flow of blood before I go.' She bent forward and began to wind the makeshift bandage tight round the wound. Saul did not protest. He was feeling sick and dizzy and he was embarrassingly close to tears, but they would have been tears of anger rather than pain.

* * *

Apart from Big Lew O'Hara standing outside the Lucky Lode, Silver Street appeared deserted at first glance. It was only when one looked closer that one would have been aware of eyes watching from windows, of men lolling against clapboard walls in the deepest shadows, of the heads above the false parapets of the flat-roofed buildings. No one spoke. The bets had been laid the night before.

Big Lew looked up and down the street. In two or three minutes it would be nine o'clock. He wondered if the boy would come, or whether the thought of the duel in the blackest hours of the night had caused him to lose heart.

The proprietor of the Silver Lode wore a loose white silk shirt, open at the throat, to allow him ease of motion when the time came to reach for the Navy Colt strapped to his thigh. He had shaved as carefully as ever and now he looked a handsome figure as he stood alone in the hot sunshine.

Up and down Silver Street the hidden onlookers peered at their watches. It was nine o'clock, the appointed hour. Seconds ticked by. In front of the saloon Big Lew began to pace up and down with the mechanical walk of a sentry. He was getting restless at the non-appearance of his adversary.

Within him the tension had built up almost to a climax. And now it seemed his taut nerves and muscles would not be able to find release in conflict.

Suddenly he stiffened. Round the corner at the far end of the street appeared a small figure. The kid had come to keep his appointment with death.

The watchers close to the corner where Saul had appeared sucked in their breath. There was something strange about the boy, his gait was unsteady and his face a sickly white. With his bleached hair blowing in the hot breeze it was as though he was without colour, apart from the two bright blue points of his eyes. There was a bandage on his right arm, a bandage which was gradually turning red.

As he walked slowly up the street the injured arm swung uselessly and he bit his bottom lip with pain.

On seeing him, Big Lew began to walk slowly forward, his eyes squinting with concentration. As the distance between him and Saul narrowed he kept his eyes focused on the boy's face—it is always the eyes that give a hint when a man is going to go for his gun.

The distance between the two men lessened and to the unseen audience time suddenly seemed to stand still. It was the endless moment before the guns of the duellists would explode in death. On an on walked Saul.

He's goddam cool, thought Big Lew. He's waiting for me. Another two paces and the distance'll be right. One ...two...

Suddenly the Navy Colt was jerked from its holster. Big Lew went into a crouch as his gun swung up. His finger contracted the trigger. But the pistol in Saul's left hand spoke first. The .44-.40 slug caught Big Lew agonisingly above his silver belt buckle.

He sagged at the knees, but even so managed to raise his gun again and fire at the youth through the red mists which were blotting out the light.

The bullet whined close to Saul's head as he fired for the second time. This bullet struck Big Lew in the heart, its impact spinning him round before he toppled full length, burying his face in the dust.

There was a long, breathless pause, then Saul took several paces forward, halted and gazed down at the body of his victim.

A small crowd gathered at a respectful distance round the tableau. Slowly the boy bolstered the gun. From its muzzle a thin blue ribbon of smoke hung in the air.

There was a scream. Several of the silent spectators were thrust aside and Melinda ran forward, dropping to her knees by the dead man.

'Lewis! Lewis!' she cried, trying to turn him over.

'T'ain't no good, ma'am,' said the town constable gently. 'He's dead an' he died in a fair fight.'

The girl looked up at Saul, standing with a strange faraway look on his pallid face.

'It's an evil thing you have done,' she cried. 'Today you have earned the mark of Cain.'

From the other side of the street Topaz approached the body. Tears were streaming down her face. 'Oh God, why did it have to happen?' she moaned. 'It's my fault—my fault. And it's too late to ask forgiveness.'

For a moment Saul's eyes rested on the two stricken women kneeling beside Big Lew before he turned and walked alone down the street. He was in pain from his wound and weak from the sudden, indescribable release of tension.

He felt sick. His first killing! And yet, above all he felt a strange secret joy. After a while he remembered the Professor and looked around for him, but he was not to be seen. He was already at the telegraph office, writing rapidly on a pad of blanks.

\* \* \*

Saul Powers and Professor Coffin rode slowly along the trail which had so recently brought them to Gila Springs.

'I know you won't feel like the journey with that arm,' the Professor had said, 'but it's best to get out of town as soon as you can after a shooting, before friends of the deceased try to even things up, or some young punk tries to grab himself some glory by shooting down the man who killed Lew O'Kara.'

Saul had agreed readily. The sight of the two women bending over the corpse in the dust kept floating before his eyes and he was anxious to get away from the town as the Professor.

'That was one of the best pieces of gunplay it has been my pleasure to report,' said the Professor. 'I never knew you could use your left hand as well as your right.'

'I guess it just seemed to come natural.'

'Tell me one thing,' said the Professor. 'Where did you get a left-handed holster from at such short notice?'

'Why, that was my father's,' Saul answered. 'Surely you must have known he was a left-handed shot?'

# CHAPTER 6

The winter rain fell like a solid curtain of water, churning the dust trail into a treacherous channel of mud. Hunched in their streaming slickers, Saul Powers and the Professor said nothing except to mutter an occasional word of encouragement to their shivering animals as they struggled up the steep path.

Eighteen months had passed since the shooting at Gila Springs. During that time Saul had spent most of his time at his mother's home at Paradise while his wounded arm slowly healed. Melinda's bullet had not only torn tendon and muscle, it had caused an infection which for some days made a doctor wonder if he should amputate in order to save his patient's life. Saul had fought against such surgery and gradually the terrible swelling subsided. Life began to throb painfully again in the crooked fingers.

At Paradise he helped his mother with her tiny farm and exercised for hours daily to get the stiffness out of his crippled limb. Fearing that it would never be supple enough to wield his Frontier again, he began training himself to shoot as well with his left hand. The Professor meanwhile had gone back East on some mysterious errand of his own.

Word of the duel with Big Lew had filtered back to Paradise, many newspapers having carried highly colourful descriptions of the encounter. Saul was something of a local celebrity. But he seemed to ignore his new fame and moodily kept himself to himself.

At last a letter came from the Professor

instructing him to meet him at the town of Railhead. He added that he had a clue to the whereabouts of Charlie Gideon. Saul saddled up and left his mother, who watched him dwindle along the eastern trail with a look of fierce pride in her burning eyes.

From Railhead the two men rode north towards the wild hill country of Nebraska where the Professor believed Gideon was leading an outlaw existence under another name. Having spent so many years roving the West in search of material he had numerous sources of information.

After they had travelled for a week the winter announced itself with torrents of chilling rain, and it was through this the two companions were riding to Caleb City, a small trail town that had grown on the edge of the ranges almost in spite of itself. It presented a dreary sight in the wet, its few streets expanses of mud and its shanty buildings silhouettes of grey in a grey world.

The Professor and Saul reined up at Caleb's only hotel, the Cattleman's Rest, and checked in. When their horses had been stabled and they had changed into dry clothes they entered the bar for some grog to kill the cold that was making their bodies tremble. A group of men were playing cards in a corner and the bartender was gloomily watching the rivulets streaming down the windows.

'What'll it be, gents?' he inquired without interest.

'Rye and hot water,' the Professor ordered.

'Twice,' said Saul. His eyes narrowed as he saw a poster above the bar.

'Where did that come from?' he asked.

## $500 Reward
will be paid for the killing or arrest of
### 'Black' Charles Gideon
six feet high, heavy black beard.
Wanted for murder and robbery.
He is always heavily armed and
has experience with explosives.

The above reward will be paid at
### The Sheriff's Office, Caleb City
on proof of his death or on his apprehension,
plus 10 per cent
of all moneys recovered.

'The sheriff asked me to put it up.'

'Where's his office?'

'Right next door.'

The sheriff looked up when the two companions walked in.

'I hear there's a five hundred dollar reward for Charlie Gideon,' said Saul bluntly.

The sheriff nodded.

'I aim to earn it. Got any idea where he hangs out?'

'You a bounty-hunter?' asked the sheriff, swinging his riding boots off the desk.

'Maybe,' said Saul. 'Let's just say I don't like Gideon.'

'Then you're not alone, son,' said the sheriff. 'I reckon he's about the most evil *hombre* ever to come into my county. If you have a grudge go after him if you must, but I warn you, he's put some mighty good men underground.'

'I'll worry about myself,' Saul said.

'My young friend is no stranger to gunplay,' said

the Professor, sensing the sheriffs resentment of this cocksure young man with his flashy, white-handled Colt strapped low on his thigh gunfighter style. 'If you could suggest where we could locate this outlaw we'd be very grateful.'

The sheriffs eyes swivelled to the tall, flabby man.

'What's your part in this, mister, you don't look like a bounty man to me...'

The Professor drew a card from his wallet and laid it on the desk, the sheriff looked at it a moment and exclaimed: 'You're the newspaper fella. Why, I've read some of them things you've wrote. Didn't you write up the life of Grant Hicks...'

'That's so. Now, I'm gathering material, as you might say. I'd be happy to know your name, sir.'

He drew out his thick leather-covered notebook.

'I'm Ford Wayne – W-A-Y-N-E,' the sheriff replied. 'Here, mister, let me offer you a drink, an' your friend. It ain't everyday we get a real newspaper man in Caleb City. Now, just tell me how I can help you an' I will – and – uh – in return maybe you could sorta mention...'

'I understand, sheriff, you just leave it to me. Now, what can you tell us about Gideon?'

'Not much. He's made things so hot for himself he has to hole up in the ranges. Sometimes he comes down when he needs supplies or money.'

The sheriff pulled out some papers from a drawer and thumbed through them. ' 'Bout a month ago he held up the Blackhill Cattlemen's and Miners' Bank. A posse followed him a long way but lost him in the ranges. From what I hear tell he's still up there, waitin' for the heat to die down.'

The sheriff spread a map on his desk and pointed to a spot with a blunt forefinger. 'It's my guess he's there

– at Crazy Bear,' he explained. 'There's a ghost settlement there, built by miners 'bout ten winters ago, but the seam ran out an' they all quit. It's a hard place to reach, just an old trail leadin' to it which could be easily guarded.'

'If you figure he's there, why ain't you gone after him?' Saul demanded.

'Waitin' for the rain to stop,' said the sheriff. 'Couldn't get up there in this weather any more'n he could get away. He'll keep, an' when it stops I've fixed to take a posse up there 'cause if I don't lay him soon this county'll be hollerin' for a new sheriff.' He laughed and downed the glass of Old Vermont he had poured himself.

'You boys are welcome to join in,' he added as Saul and the Professor raised their glasses.

'That'd be fine,' said the Professor. 'We'll stay at the Cattleman's Rest until the rain clears. It should make a very good story.'

'You bet it will,' said the sheriff with enthusiasm. 'The killin' of Charlie Gideon'll be talked about for years to come. Good day, gents – an' don't forget my name has a Y, an' an E at the end.'

'I ain't gonna wait for that old stumblebum to get a posse together,' said Saul when they left the office. 'I'm gonna go after Charlie Gideon now. He's my meat an' I ain't figurin' on sharin' him.'

'That would be madness,' said the Professor. 'You'll never find him in this rain. All you'd do is get lost and make a fool of yourself. You don't know this territory, it's very tricky. Besides, if he's holed up in a good vantage point it'll take more than one man to get him.'

'That's my idea of goin' now,' replied Saul impatiently. 'He'd never expect anyone to go after him in this weather. I tell you, I'm goin' up to Crazy Bear today.'

'No you aren't,' said the Professor. 'I'm telling

you not to go. You do the shooting and I do the planning, wasn't that the deal?'

'Maybe you think it'd be a better story if Charlie Gideon made a last stand against a whole posse...'

The Professor looked at Saul with a curious bleak smile on his large face. Saul couldn't see his eyes behind the blue tinted glasses, but he could imagine their expression.

'Don't say anything like that again,' he said softly. 'You don't know anything except gun handling. Just remember you're the hand of vengeance – I'm the brain. If it wasn't for me you'd still be in Paradise hoeing your Ma's bean patch...'

'Okay, Professor,' Saul muttered. 'You're the boss.'

\* \* \*

There was a grin on Saul's face as he pushed the badly written, misspelled note under the door of the Professor's room. Then, moving like a cat and carrying his Winchester in his hand, he walked down the corridor and through the wet darkness to the stables. Here in the light of the smoky oil lamp he saddled up his horse, slipped the rifle into its saddle sheath and rode quietly away from the Cattleman's Rest.

In the east the darkness began to lose its intensity and soon there was enough watery light for Saul to pick out the trail which led away from Caleb City.

After his meeting with the sheriff yesterday he had spent the rest of the time playing poker with some of the regulars in the bar of the Cattleman's Rest. Not only had he come out of the long game a few dollars richer, but, through casual conversation, had learnt something of the topography of the locality.

Soon the trail forked. He took the left-hand branch which soon narrowed and became more and more uneven. It was a trail that had not been in use for a long time, for this was the way to the half-forgotten ghost town of Crazy Bear high in the forbidding ranges.

Saul continued along this track at a walk. To have gone faster would have been impossible over the sodden ground. Rain drummed against his broad-brimmed hat and trickled down his slicker, and soon he was as cold as when he and the Professor had ridden into Caleb City the day before.

Towards the evening he found a dilapidated shack standing some yards from the track. It had not been used for many years and its warped shingled roof sagged alarmingly. Nevertheless it was shelter and Saul led his horse in through the doorway! His first job was to rub down the shivering animal and in doing so he restored his own circulation.

The animal nuzzled him with affection when he placed a canvas bucket of oats before it. Next he spread out his damp blankets and, sitting cross-legged, opened a can of beans which he ate cold. Having finished his depressing supper, he explored the room again to make sure the wet had not forced any reptiles to take shelter there. Then, to the sounds of endlessly dripping water, and the contented champing of his mount, he rolled himself in his blankets. He laid the Winchester beside him and kept his hand on the smooth bone butt of the Colt Frontier. Within minutes he was asleep.

Next morning Saul saw the rain had lessened to a drizzle. Leaving the old shack he found the trail became steeper and in parts he had to dismount and lead his horse. From what he had gathered from the poker players, the ghost town was only a further five miles into the ranges from the cabin where he had passed the night.

Apparently the last part of the trail was so steep that it was practically impossible to ride up it. At the top it passed through a cleft in weather-worn cliffs which opened into a small valley where Crazy Bear was situated.

As there was no other entrance one rifleman at the top of the trail could keep back an army.

Saul doubted if Charlie Gideon was at the ghost town he would bother to guard the trail in such foul conditions. He was pinning his hopes on finding his quarry in one of the old shacks that had been left by the long-gone miners.

Visibility was bad in the drizzle but now the trail was becoming so steep that Saul recognised his closeness to the deserted settlement. The time had come for him to leave his horse.

It took him about an hour to find a suitable place. Having left the trail, he finally came upon a cave-like entrance in a rocky slope. Two decaying wooden railway lines vanished into subterranean darkness, indicating that this had once been an entrance to a mine. Saul led the horse inside and tethered it to an old sleeper. Here at least it would be hidden from view and protected from the weather. Saul filled its bucket to the top with oats and then continued on his journey by foot, the Winchester slung across his back.

It was noon by the time he reached a point on the trail where he could see the V-shaped gap in the cliff which led to Crazy Bear. Just in case the wanted outlaw had taken it into his head to watch the trail, Saul now left it and began scrambling through patches of dwarf oak and up steep stony slopes so he could approach the cleft from the side.

When he reached the narrow ledge level with the opening, he paused to get his breath and unsling his rifle. Cautiously he edged his way along the base of the cliffs to where the trail vanished.

He had to move with extreme caution. Not only was he afraid of giving himself away should Gideon be on guard, but he also had to watch his footing. The ledge became extremely narrow and the rock that made it up was so rotten that frequently pieces broke off under his riding boots and went rolling down the slope.

Several times Saul was in danger of plunging over the edge, but finally he managed to inch himself to the gap. He peered round a shoulder of rock. The narrow pass seemed deserted. Beyond it in the mist he could just make out the hidden valley and the indistinct shape of the ghost town.

With his Colt in one hand and the rifle in the other, he walked through the passage until he found himself in the oval-shaped valley, the walls of which showed several black entrances of disused mines similar to the one where he had left his horse.

The ghost town itself was a depressing huddle of crazily angled shacks. One or two had fallen down completely. The rest were in various stages of disrepair.

Saul crouched behind a slab of rock and surveyed the scene intently for a long time. If Charlie Gideon was there, which of the shacks would be sheltering him? Somewhere a door swung on rusty hinges, giving forth a high-pitched screech that made Saul grit his teeth. Then his ears caught another sound, the distant whicker of a horse. Like Saul, the outlaw must have used a mine tunnel as a stable. At least this was confirmation that he was close at hand.

Moving like a shadow in the rain, Saul bent double and approached the nearest of the shacks. With infinite care he stepped on to its verandah and looked through the doorway. The interior was empty apart from an old stove red with rust. A long time had passed since any human being had stayed here. Saul moved on to the next one.

Suddenly a shot rang out, splintering the decaying woodwork a few inches above his head. By reflex action Saul threw himself round a corner and flattened himself hard against the clap-board. In the drizzle he could not see where the shot had come from, but he guessed it had not been from any of the old buildings. Most likely Charlie Gideon had been in one of the tunnels with his horse when Saul arrived. Perhaps he had even watched him make his reconnaissance over the barrel of a gun.

Not knowing where the next shot might come from, Saul began to work his way down the narrow alley that led between the derelict buildings. As he turned the corner of the last shack, the unseen rifle cracked again. A bullet must have struck something hard for it gave a high whine of a ricochet. Saul jumped back to shelter.

This last shot had given him an indication of the whereabouts of his adversary. Clearly he was not among the buildings of the ghost town, but in one of the old mine workings in the opposite cliff. Quickly Saul entered a cabin, which seemed a little stouter than the rest, and crossed the floor to the window which gave a view of the valley floor. He took off his slicker to allow himself more freedom, bolstered the Colt and slipped the barrel of the Winchester across the window ledge. Through the fine rain he could see an upturned miner's truck at one of the tunnel entrances.

He thought he glimpsed a grey figure crouched behind it. The Winchester spat and Saul had the satisfaction of seeing the distant shadow vanish. A few seconds later Saul thought he detected movement again. He saw a brief stab of yellow flame and then a heavy bullet whistled through the opening, perilously close to his head. Smoke from his rifle must have given away his position at the window. Several more slugs followed in quick succession. Then there was silence.

Anxious to draw his enemy's fire, Saul took off his hat and hung it at the end of his rifle barrel. Slowly he poked this above the window sill. Immediately the crash of a rifle echoed in the small valley. A bullet plucked the hat off the barrel and sent it spinning across the room.

Saul dropped to his hands and knees and scrabbled across the floor, wondering if his trick had worked. Would Charlie Gideon think he had scored a hit? To add to the effect he gave a mighty cry as though in mortal agony. Reaching a doorway he jumped through it and eased his way to the corner of the house where he could see the opening of the mineworks.

The ruse had not fooled the outlaw. If Saul had expected to see him walk into the open after the scream he was disappointed.

Carefully he sighted the rifle on the old truck. If its woodwork was in the same condition as the shacks of Crazy Bear, there was a good chance he would be able to pump bullets right through it. He squeezed the trigger and saw chunks of rotten wood burst from its side under the impact of the bullet.

There was no reply to Saul's shot. Could it be that Charlie Gideon had caught the bullet after it had passed through the truck? Or was he lying doggo, playing the same game as Saul had played? Saul was determined not to take chances. Raising the rifle again, he put shot after shot into the truck. Still there was no reply. He wriggled back and then moved to another vantage point behind an old cauldron. Once more he fired and once more splinters flew but again there was no response from his enemy.

Cupping his hands to his mouth, he shouted, 'Charlie Gideon, if you give yourself up, I'll let you stand trial fair and square at Caleb City.' The words echoed eerily, but there was no reply except for the drip, drip, drip of water running off the eaves of the ghost town.

Then, despite the cold, Saul broke into a light sweat. He cursed himself for thinking his enemy might still be behind the makeshift barricade at the cave mouth. No doubt there was a whole network of tunnels. While he had been blazing away it was possible that Charlie Gideon was making his way through subterranean passages so he could surprise the intruder from the rear.

As this thought struck him Saul jumped to his feet, ready to face trouble from any direction. But he was too late. Something seemed to explode against the back of his head with tremendous force. Momentarily a blinding light seared his brain before it was extinguished by a merciful rush of darkness. The Winchester dropped from his nerveless fingers. His knees buckled, then he was lying face down in the mud, oblivious to the hoarse laughter of his unseen assailant.

## CHAPTER 7

When Saul opened his eyes he had the sensation of being in a nightmare. Before his eyes was a terrifying face like that of an ogre from childhood's grimmest fancies. It had a great mane of tangled hair and a matted beard which grew up to small, pig-like eyes. A gash suddenly appeared in the beard, a gash full of broken blackened teeth.

'An' who the hell are you?' demanded Charlie Gideon.

Looking past the terrible face, Saul saw a broken roof above him. He was lying stretched out on the floor of one of Crazy Bear's abandoned cabins. He tried to move, but the effect was agonising. Not only did burning pains shoot through his head where he had been pistol whipped, but there was a dull throbbing in his ankles and in his wrists. His captor had tightened the thongs until they bit deep into his flesh.

'I'm askin' – who the hell are ya?'

'Just a stranger passin' through,' muttered Saul weakly.

'No one ever passes through Crazy Bear. Where's your hoss?'

'Broke its pastern, had to shoot it,' lied Saul.

'Ya're lyin'. Save yourself tribulation an' tell me who ya are. If ya don't I'll get it outa ya in two minutes flat. I know some Sioux tricks that'll make ya think death is the sweetest thing under the sun. Are you a bounty man – have ya come after the five hundred dollar price that's on my head?'

Saul shook his head. 'It ain't the bounty,' he muttered.

'You a spy then – is a posse comin'?'

'Sure there's a posse comin'. There'll always be a posse comin' for a coyote like you...'

Charlie Gideon laughed harshly and stood up. From the sound of his laughter Saul realised he was not only in the hands of a homicidal outlaw but a madman. Clad in filthy fringed buckskins, his hair flowing over his shoulders, he looked more like an ogre than ever, especially as his height was well over six feet and his body was broad in proportion.

'So you're a lousy, goddam spy,' he muttered. 'You figured I wouldn't be keepin' a look out in the rain. When's the posse comin'?'

Automatically Saul's eyes shifted to the window. The rain had stopped.

Charlie Gideon chuckled. 'Sure, the weather's changed, so I guess they'll be on their way. Well, they'll get a reception they ain't planned on. From the top of the trail I could hold back the whole United States army.'

He slapped his Spencer rifle. 'I'm gonna go an' wait for 'em now,' he continued. 'As for you, you can stay here awhile. Maybe you'll be useful to me as a hostage, or maybe I'll just slit your throat when I need some fun.' Again he laughed.

Suddenly his heavily booted foot lashed out at Saul, and once more the young man sank into oblivion.

\* \* \*

It was the distant echo of a rifle shot that roused Saul again. He did not know how long he had lain unconscious, but now the pain in his wrists and ankles made him break into a sweat.

There was the sound of a muffled sob, and moving his head slightly he saw the figure of a girl sitting on the floor close to him. Like Charlie Gideon, her long hair was unkempt, though beneath the film of dirt on her face her features showed that they had been pretty once. Over her shoulders she wore an old army greatcoat, beneath it was a ragged dress that normally would not have been fit for a scarecrow. Seeing Saul's eyes move she held her fingers up to her lips.

'Don't you holler out none,' she pleaded. 'He'd whup the hide offa my bones if he came an' found me here.'

Her accent was strange and coarse, and Saul guessed she must have been the daughter of a rawhider, one of those poverty-stricken gipsies who roamed the remoter parts 'of the West in broken-down wagons held together by strips of rawhide. A breed of their own, they wandered restlessly, suffering any hardship to avoid regular work. Maverick meat supplied their food, and if some of the 'mavericks' had a brand it did not matter. Travellers avoided their untidy camps, with their squalling brats and prematurely aged, bitter-eyed women. These outcasts were bad medicine.

'Who are you?' whispered Saul.

'My name is Virtue,' the trembling girl replied.

'What are you doin' here?'

'Charlie Gideon brought me here, mister. He took me from my Pa's wagon one night. Honest, I didn't want to come, he's misused me somethin' cruel he has. I was a good girl till he stole me off. He held up the wagon with his gun an' he made Pa give him food. All we had was some maize meal but he took that. He was on the run, see, mister. Then he made me get up on his hoss, an' Pa ran to get his ole gun, but Charlie he fired an' wounded him an' rode off with me. An' I been here ever since.'

'Do you stay in one of these cabins?' asked Saul.

'No, mister, Charlie's too cunnin' for that. He fixed up in one of them ole mine tunnels. If he were attacked he could always get away down the passage. But it's dark in there, mister, an' it spooks me awful. Sometimes I creep out to look at the sky. If he finds me he whups me...'

Saul saw two large tears were running down her face, leaving pale trails in the grime.

'If you could set me free, Virtue, I could get you away from here. Cut the thongs and give me my gun.'

She shook her head.

'I ain't that crazy. You'll never get away from Charlie alive. There ain't nothin' I can do for you mister. Why, if he found me here he'd near kill me. Once I tried to get away an' he caught me an' tied me up for two days in the mine shaft. He took away the lamp an' the rats came...' she shuddered. 'If you was my own kin I couldn't help you. 'Sides, I ain't even got a knife an' rawhide knots just can't be untied. I must go now, if he comes back...'

She stood up and Saul noticed she was barefooted.

'Virtue, you'll be all right. I'll kill Charlie, an' then I'll take you back to town an' buy you a new dress an' shoes, an' an elegant bonnet...'

'That's just talk, mister,' said the girl. 'You couldn't kill Charlie, nothin' except Almighty God could strike him down. It's a pity, cause I sure would like a dress – an' shoes...! ain't never had none.'

'I saw some mighty pretty shoes down in Caleb City,' said Saul. 'An' there was a dress in a store – my, oh my, it sure was a fine dress...'

'What colour?' demanded the girl, her whining voice suddenly eager.

'It was sorta blue,' said Saul. 'Blue – like the sky, an' it was made of silk an' ...an' it sorta shone all soft like when the light hit it...'

'You ain't makin' this up, mister.'

'No,' lied Saul. 'It must have come from the

East, this dress. It had a sorta sash. You'd sure look superior in that dress, Virtue.'

'Tell me about the shoes,' she urged.

'Waal, the shoes were – uh – made of – uh – leather...'

'All shiny black?'

'Yeah, that's right – all shiny black, an' they had silver buckles on them.'

'An' what else...'

'Waal, I guess that's all. Shoes is shoes, but those shoes I seen were better than any other shoes I ever laid eyes on afore.'

'It ain't no good,' said Virtue, banishing a secret dream. 'You an' I'll never get away from Crazy Bear...'

'Goddam it, girl, we could if you'd set me free,' cried Saul angrily. 'I guess in your heart you don't want to leave...'

'That's a wicked lie, mister. It's just that I know Charlie Gideon an' he's ole Satan hisself...'

Saul suddenly moaned as a wave of pain swept over him.

'You got any water?' he muttered.

Fearfully Virtue looked round her, then slipped from the room. Saul wondered if she would return, but she did and gently put a rusted bean can of muddy water to his lips.

Greedily he swallowed it.

'Thanks,' he said gratefully. 'You're an angel to do that.'

'I ain't no angel,' she whined. 'Charlie Gideon made me a bad girl. When I die I'll go to hell an''...'

There came the sound of shots and then silence.

'What's that?' demanded Saul.

'I dunno. Maybe Charlie's huntin'. He goes huntin' for squirrels an' rabbits an' things...'

'That ain't huntin', there were too many shots,'

said Saul excitedly. 'I know what that is. It's Sheriff Wayne's posse come up from Caleb City...'

A look of fear crossed Virtue's face. 'I must get back to the tunnel,' she said. 'There'll be killin'. Charlie will kill them all. No one could get up that trail against his gun, an' he's got blastin' powder as well.'

'Blastin' powder?'

'Yes, I saw him fillin' ole airtights an' puttin' fuses in. He told me that if a posse came he could blow them offa the side of the mountain.. .An' he treats me awful when he's been killin' – it does somethin' to him.'

'If you could release me, I could go up an' take him from behind,' said Saul. 'Come on, girl. Now's your chance to get away from all this. You can go back to your folks and forget all this...'

Her lip curled bitterly. 'They wouldn't take me back nohow,' she said. ''Sides, I wouldn't know where to find them.'

'Waal, you could live at Caleb City an' wear that blue dress and them fancy shoes...'

'You sure about that dress? Is it as blue as the sky...'

'It surely is... a summer sky.' Suddenly the strange wild girl made up her mind. 'You'd fix it for me,' she said.

'Surely.'

'What's your name?'

'Saul Powers.'

'All right, Saul Powers I'll try.' She looked at the bonds on his ankles. 'I ain't got a knife,' she said, her voice returning to its natural whine. 'Ain't no good without a knife.'

'The airtight, the one you gave me the drink in. Could you use that...'

'I've got a better idea. Roll on your side, Saul Powers.'

He did so, and bending down she began to bite at the leather thongs on his wrists.

Minutes passed, and the sound of gunfire became more frequent. Saul could imagine the posse spread out on the steep trail behind what cover they could find, while Charlie Gideon, well hidden, aimed the .56-50 calibre Spencer at the slightest movement.

Suddenly the thongs went slack and Saul moved his wrists apart. As the blood began to pulse again the pain became even more intense. He sat up and began to rub his purple flesh, aghast at the deep furrows that crisscrossed it. Meanwhile Virtue was at work on the strips that bound his ankles.

Minutes later Saul was able to stagger to his feet. He felt so giddy that he reeled against the wall. Virtue cringed away from him, obviously terrified at what she had done.

'My gun,' murmured Saul as the vertigo left him.

'Charlie took it,' she answered. 'He don't leave any weapon around. Maybe he's scared I'd get it an' use it on him.'

Saul swore under his breath. With his body only under partial control and without his beloved Colt Frontier, it seemed he stood little chance against the heavily armed killer.

'You stay here,' he told, Virtue. 'If there's any shootin' lay flat on the floor an' no harm will come to you.'

She nodded miserably.

'You ain't gonna forget your words...'

'What...'

'What you said about that there sky blue gown...'

An unaccustomed feeling of pity filled him.

'Don't you fret none, Virtue,' he said soothingly, putting his arm round her thin shoulders. 'When this is over, you'll have your dress an' shoes and you'll be the belle of Caleb City. Now, I've got work to do.'

He stumbled out of the cabin and began to walk between the ruined buildings towards the sound of gunfire.

Often he stumbled as his legs refused to work properly and once he had to sit down on the step of what had once been the Crazy Bear store. Bending down, he sluiced his face with water from a puddle and then he felt better.

Soon he left the ghost settlement and began moving across the floor of the valley towards the cleft in the towering cliffs. He had looked in vain for some sort of weapon. Now he stooped down and picked up a heavy stone, reflecting as he did so that it would be of very little use against a heavy rifle.

As he went forward cautiously he tried to remember the lie of the ground at the top of the trail. There were several half-buried boulders just outside the cleft. Doubtless Gideon would be lying behind one of these. If only he could find a way of climbing above him he could have the advantage of dropping down on him, or even throwing a rock down on him. The one thing in his favour was that the last thing the outlaw would expect would be an attack from behind.

As he approached the narrow opening in the cliff wall, he noticed that its sides were scarred with cracks and fissures. Mentally cursing his clumsy fingers, Saul placed his stone in the large hip pocket of his Levis and began to climb up the left wall of the cleft, gradually working his way from handhold to handhold.

The rifle fire continued intermittently. Several times spent bullets whined high above his head. At last he reached a tiny ledge that ran horizontally along the wall. Inch by inch he worked his way along this, his body flat against the rock and his arms stretched out as though trying to embrace it. If his ankles let him down now it would be fatal.

After some minutes he rounded the shoulder of the cliff and found himself looking down on the entrance to the Crazy Bear Valley. He had a panoramic view of the hillside which sloped steeply down to a rolling carpet of forest. He could see the trail clearly, and make out the tiny figures of the posse scattered behind scanty cover on each side of it.

Directly below him he saw the hulking body of Charlie Gideon on the flat top of a boulder. He had a rifle at his shoulder, while a revolver and several canisters lay in readiness in front of him.

As he watched, Saul noticed one of the members of the posse begin to worm forward from the rock outcrop behind which he had been crouching. It was obvious that Charlie Gideon saw the movement too. He moved the barrel of his rifle slightly and waited. Saul knew he had to act fast if he was to save the unknown man. Placing the fingers of his left hand into a narrow crevice, he tried to pull the stone out of his pocket. It had been a squeeze to get it in, now it seemed impossible to get it out with his swollen fingers. In his efforts he almost lost his precarious foothold, and for several tense seconds he had to cling to the wet rock with both hands.

Meanwhile the man below snaked from cover to cover, no doubt hoping to get near enough to the hidden rifleman to be able to surprise him. He little realised that his every move was being watched over the Spencer's sights. He reached the last twenty yards of the trail. Here the ground was steep and completely devoid of cover. He stood up, and as though at a prearranged signal the rest of the posse blazed away in the hope of pinning the sniper down. The bullets sang and ricocheted round the boulders at the top of the trail, while the deputy began to scramble up the steep slope.

Contemptuous of the flying lead, Charlie Gideon

raised his head slightly and squeezed the trigger. The bullet struck the man full in the chest. With a grunt he staggered back, then rolled over and over down the trail.

The firing died down as the corpse came to rest spread-eagled on the muddy track. Below him Saul saw Charlie Gideon calmly reloading. Again he tried to get the stone out of his pocket, but found it impossible with his semi-paralysed hand.

It seemed an impasse. In his positon flattened against the rock wall Saul was powerless to do anything to help the posse which in turn was pinned down by Gideon's deadly Spencer.

Then the vague murmur of voices floated up. Down on the trail Sheriff Wayne was giving an order to the man nearest to him. This was passed on to the next and so on until it reached every man crouched on the wet hillside.

Suddenly, and with great bravery, the peace officer rose from behind the rotten tree trunk which years before had rolled down the mountain during a blizzard. He fired his pistol above his head, and as he did so ten men rose as one. It was obvious that they were going to try and take Charlie Gideon by a suicidal charge.

# CHAPTER 8

Firing as they went, the posse from Caleb City started up the slope. Sheriff Wayne had gambled on the sudden charge bewildering Gideon. He would not be able to pick them all off, especially as they were widely scattered, and he would have to expose himself if he planned on driving them back with a fusillade of shots. But, to his surprise, Saul saw the outlaw lay aside his rifle as the men toiled towards him. He seized a canister and struck a match with his left hand.

Sporadic shots left snail's trails of hot lead on the rocks as the attackers came closer, but Charlie Gideon did not reply. Instead he lit the fuse that dangled from his grenade. Sparks hissed as it began its deadly journey towards the compressed blasting powder.

In a frenzy, Saul clawed at his pocket. If he could not get the stone out, perhaps he could rip the patch pocket off and get it that way. As he tugged with his free hand, he yelled: 'Get back, boys...'

The outlaw was so concentrating on the fuse, waiting for the exact moment to hurl his home made bomb, that he did not look up. But the men of the posse gazed up in surprise, seeing the small figure of Saul high on the cliff for the first time.

The copper rivets holding the pocket suddenly gave, and as the fine canvas tore away, Saul's fingers closed on his stone. At that moment Charlie Gideon stood up to lob the canister which had hardly any fuse left.

With all his strength Saul hurled the stone at the

big outlaw. It struck him hard on the side of the head. In pain and surprise he reeled back, dropping the bomb. For a second he watched it lying on the boulder, then he turned and bounded into the cleft. Saul closed his eyes and pressed himself against the cliff...

Next instant the bomb exploded with a roar which echoed and re-echoed in the valley. A great tongue of lurid flame spouted up, followed by a billowing cloud of smoke. The blast prised Saul from his perch and sent him slithering down the cliff through the black acrid fog.

By a miracle he missed the boulders which had sheltered the outlaw, and he found himself suddenly in the light again, rolling over and over down the muddy trail until he slithered to a stop in the middle of the amazed posse.

'I'll be gosh darned,' exclaimed Sheriff Wayne. 'You look like you come outa a minstrel show.' The rest of the men guffawed at Saul's blackened appearance.

'Waal, I guess that's the end of Charlie Gideon,' said one. 'Guess we oughta thank you, Powers, for stoppin' that there grenade comin' our way.'

'Don't thank me yet,' Saul replied, rubbing his inflamed eyes. 'That blast never killed him. I saw him run back into the cleft just before it went off. For my money he's back at Crazy Bear right now.'

'Let's mosey up an' take a look,' said the sheriff. 'An' keep your shootin' irons ready, boys, that *hombre* is more poison than a stateful of rattlers.'

At that moment the group was joined by a tall bulky figure with blue tinted spectacles. Obviously the Professor had been covering the battle from the shelter of the forest.

'Howdy, Professor,' said Saul. 'I guess you musta got my note.'

'I got it all right,' the journalist replied sourly. 'I hope you've learned your lesson. It's a wonder you're still alive.'

'Well, I am,' said Saul. 'But I'll bet you had my obituary ready.'

'That's always ready,' the Professor retorted.

The men began to move up the slope. At the top they found the twisted remains of Gideon's Spencer and revolver, but there was no sign of the outlaw.

'Well, he'll have to fight with his hands,' said the sheriff, hopefully.

'I wouldn't be too sure, he's got my Winchester stashed away somewheres,' said Saul. 'An' he's got my Colt, too, goddam him. I'd sure be hurt to lose that gun.'

Cautiously the men filed into the narrow pass. When they were through they fanned out and covered the collection of derelict buildings with their weapons.

Suddenly there was a sharp crack and a high whine.

'That's the Winchester,' muttered Saul grimly as he threw himself flat.

From each side of him came a roar of gunfire as the posse replied by sending a wild volley into the ghost town.

'Watch your aim, boys,' Saul cried. There's a girl somewheres in there.'

'Yeah, an' there's also a man with five hundred bucks on his head,' said the man next to him.

Again the Winchester spat and the man who had just spoken yelped in agony. A thick ribbon of smoke drifted from the window of the nearest shack.

The posse fired again and chunks of rotten wood jumped from the wall as the bullets hammered home.

'He won't last in there,' grunted the sheriff. 'Keep firin' boys – I'll see the County pays for the ammunition.'

Thus encouraged the men blazed away until the valley was ringing with the pandemonium of their guns.

Saul crawled across to the wounded man. His face was twisted and he had his hand to his right shoulder. Blood was oozing from between his fingers.

'Hey, fella, you won't need your gun for a while,' said Saul. 'Give it to me and maybe I'll get Gideon for you.'

'Take it,' mouthed the injured man. Saul reached across and picked up the fallen Peacemaker. He carefully wiped the blood from the butt and then tested its weight. Being different only in bore from his own gun, he had no anxiety about his ability to use it.

'Thanks, pal,' he said and began to crawl forward through the rank, wet grass covering the valley floor. Above his head the bullets of the posse continued to whine.

'At this rate they'll shoot Crazy Bear to pieces,' he muttered to himself.

Then he was aware of someone beside him.

'Gosh darn it, this ain't no place for you, Professor,' he said. 'You ain't a fightin' man.'

'No, but I want to be in at the kill,' said the big man with his mirthless smile. 'Why, there hasn't been a stand made like this since Buckshot Roberts held off the Tunstall-McSween mob at Blazer's Mill in the Lincoln County war.'

There was a yell and a renewed burst of fire. Saul looked up to see a lumbering figure run from the shelter of the old miners' cabins and head across the open ground towards the black entrance of a mine working. It seemed as though the outlaw had a charmed existence, for, despite the bullets that whistled about him, he reached the opening without injury.

'We got him bottled up now,' Sheriff Wayne shouted. 'If the worst comes to the worst we can starve the blamed critter out.'

'Don't lay no bets on that,' said Saul. 'We ain't

dealin' with a natural man.'

Then he went across to Crazy Bear, the Professor following. Anxiously he looked into several of the bullet-riddled shacks before he found Virtue crouched behind the counter of the old store. Her eyes were rolling like those of a terrified animal.

'He ain't dead yet,' she moaned. 'He'll come an' get me again...' Her whole body shuddered with fear.

'No he won't,' said Saul. 'He's gone into that old mine,' and he pointed through a window, whose frame still held fragments of shattered glass. 'Tell me, does it connect up with any of the other tunnels?'

'I don't rightly know,' the girl whined. 'But you'll never get him now...'

As she spoke there was an explosion which shook the sagging building. A great sheet of flame gushed from the mine mouth. It was followed by a sinister subterranean rumble.

'He's blocked the way in with blasting powder,' the Professor exclaimed. 'He's entombed himself!'

Leaving Virtue with the Professor, Saul ran over to where the posse was gathering in front of the mine.

'I guess he musta finished hisself off,' said the sheriff. 'He musta figured it was a better way to go than on the end of a rope. An' I reckon he was right at that.'

'No, he knows the workin's like the back of his hand,' said Saul. 'There's a maze of tunnels here...' and he went on to describe how he had been covering a mine opening while Gideon had managed to get out by another passage and come up behind him.

'We could send back to Caleb for powder an' blow up all the entrances,' mused the sheriff.

'Even that mightn't work,' said Saul. 'It could be there's a tunnel that comes out somewheres outside this valley. The girl he kidnapped – Virtue – said he planned on escapin' in the tunnels if he was attacked here.'

Sheriff Wayne scratched his head.

'There's only one way to make sure,' said Saul, 'an' that's to go after him.'

'I couldn't ask any man to go into the bowels of the earth with that coldblooded killer mebbe waitin' in the dark.'

'You don't have to ask any man, I'll go. You've gotta hunt him because you're County Sheriff – me, I gotta better reason. Look, that entrance ain't completely blocked. I guess a man could squeeze between the top of that rubble an' the roof. Anyways, I'm gonna try...'

Before anyone could argue, Saul began climbing the rubble until he was crouching against the rock roof. Then with the Peacemaker in his hand, he crawled painfully forward into the utter darkness over the debris.

The opening narrowed. Soon his back was scraping against the rock above. He had the feeling of being buried alive. An instinct told him that somewhere ahead Charlie Gideon was still alive, waiting like a trapped beast in the blackness of the mine. A man like him would never throw in his hand as the sheriff had suggested.

On the other hand Saul decided he would be some distance away. He would have retreated well out of reach of the explosion before the charge had detonated.

After some time the way became easier to the crawling man. He had passed the peak of the rubble, and was now crawling on the downward slope.

Soon he was able to stand up. He moved slightly to the right until his outstretched hand touched the damp wall. His foot struck one of the old wooden lines on which the small mine trucks had been wheeled.

Saul rested for a minute to regain his breath. He strained his ears, but all he could hear was the heavy beat of his own pulse. Then he began to move forward, foot by foot.

The darkness was ultimate. He had the sensation that it was pressing against him as though it had substance. Once he thought he heard a noise and froze, but it was only the irregular drip of water falling after seeping through the roof.

A little later his foot brushed against something which seemed like a bundle of sticks. He felt down cautiously and touched bones, probably the skeleton of an animal which had wandered into this terrifying catacomb. No wonder Virtue had risked so much to come out to look at the sky.

Minutes passed. Saul continued on as silently as he could. At length he fancied he saw a gleam of light. He wondered if his eyes had begun to play tricks, then he turned a corner and saw the tunnel widened into a fair-sized cavern. In the centre of its floor stood a kerosene lamp burning with a steady yellow flame.

Immediately he ducked back, momentarily blinded by the glow after the Stygian dark. As he did so there was a stab of fire ahead and a bullet splattered against the rock close to him. Obviously Charlie Gideon had lit the lamp there to give him the advantage over any pursuers.

Saul crouched low and, with the Peacemaker already raised, sprang round the corner and fired at the lamp. There was a tinkle of glass and the endless night of the mine closed in. Several bullets whined down the tunnel, but they passed harmlessly over Saul who was wriggling forward full length on the floor. He was able to keep his sense of direction by touching the wooden rails that ran beside him.

Suddenly he paused and listened. There was a slight scraping sound up the tunnel. Without realising why he did it, he threw up the Peacemaker and fired straight ahead of him. In the brief flash he saw a terrifying sight. A few feet ahead of him Charlie Gideon was crawling towards him with a Bowie knife in his hand.

As the echoes of the shot died Saul heard harsh breathing from the outlaw. He fired again, and in the split second of illumination saw that Gideon was even closer.

Saul almost panicked. He was pretty sure that he had hit the shaggy outlaw, yet he was still coming on. It was as though he was immune to bullets.

Hastily the young man got to his feet and backed away. The breathing was hoarser now, and closer.

'I'm gonna cut you down, man,' came the echoing voice of the outlaw. 'You'll never leave this mine alive.'

'You're wrong, Gideon,' called Saul, still backing and acutely aware his gun was half empty. I've come a mighty long way to settle an account. Remember Luke Powers, the man you killed one morning thirteen years ago? Today he's gonna have his revenge.'

The words faded into silence. In the blackness Gideon was slowly getting to his feet. Then, holding his knife in front of him, he rushed down the tunnel, catching Saul by surprise.

In an instant his left arm encircled the slim body of his enemy while with his right hand he strove to drive home the knife. In the struggle Saul managed to grasp his wrist, just keeping the deadly blade away while he fought to free his right arm to raise the Peacemaker.

For several seconds they stood like statues, neither able to move because of the grip of the other. Then Saul felt his strength ebbing. The blade of the Bowie was coming closer. Charlie Gideon chuckled in insane triumph, but the laugh became an animal shriek. In a despairing effort Saul had managed to drag his gun hand free and press the muzzle of the Colt into Gideon's sagging belly. He emptied the gun in rapid succession. The duel in the dark was over.

\* \* \*

Saul Powers and Sheriff Ford Wayne led the cavalcade slowly down the trail to Caleb City. At its rear there were two riderless horses. Over one was slung the body of the deputy who had been shot on the slope, over the other was the bloodied, bullet-riddled corpse of Charlie Gideon. Behind these two gruesome loads rode the Professor, busily writing in his leather-covered notebook.

'I can't figure why he should have come at you with a knife,' the sheriff was saying.

'Waal, he lost his guns when the blast went off at the cleft,' said Saul. 'Back at Crazy Bear he got my guns, but he hadn't any ammunition for them. I guess that's why he decided to go into the tunnel. He used the last of his bullets firin' at me in the dark. After that he had to use the knife.'

'He sure took a lot of killin',' muttered the sheriff. For a while they rode on, each busy with their thoughts. Rain had started to fall again.

'What will happen to her?' asked Saul, nodding to where Virtue sat forlorn on a horse behind them.

'Guess she'll end up in the Red Light Dance Hall,' said the sheriff indifferently. 'There ain't nothin' else for her.'

'Listen, sheriff,' said Saul, 'as I killed Charlie Gideon, I guess I collect that five hundred bucks.'

'Reckon you do.'

'Well, give it to her.'

'You crazy?'

'Just do as I say – an' tell me, sheriff...'

'Now what?'

'...is there a place in Caleb where a fella can buy a sky blue dress?'

# CHAPTER 9

It was a high-sky, spring morning. Saul felt a lightness of heart as he followed the trail which wound along the wide valley floor between high buttes of red sandstone. Since the shooting of Charlie Gideon the previous winter he had grown more accustomed to his role as a gunfighter, to the curious looks he received when he rode into a new town, or the strange atmosphere which descended when he walked into a saloon.

On two occasions he had been involved in shooting affrays. Both times the affair had started because of his reputation. Once a half drunken teamster had made a clumsy draw in a bar to prove that he was as good as any 'Kid from Paradise' (as several newspapers had begun to call him), but it turned out to be the last draw he ever made. Saul had smashed his gun hand with a .44-40 bullet.

The second time was more dangerous. Saul was in a hotel room when the door opened stealthily and a wild eyed youth crept in. Saul was shaving and noticed the movement of the door in a mirror. Whirling round, he had the bone-handled Frontier ready as the fame-hungry youth opened fire. Both guns spoke as one. The bullet fanned Saul's lathered cheek and smashed the mirror behind him, but the would-be assassin was hurled back through the door by the impact of Saul's shot.

He was carried away by his friends in a badly wounded condition. As Saul and the Professor were continuing their journey that day, Saul never knew if he lived or died.

This incident emphasised the need to carry arms at all times except when he was in bed, and then he slept with the Colt making a hard but reassuring lump beneath his pillow. This was the price he had to pay for his growing reputation, but it was a price he did not grudge.

Physically he had changed since he first left Paradise to begin his trail of vengeance. He was taller, his body had filled out and even the Professor no longer referred to him as 'boy.' When he rode into a town it was not only the male citizens who cast speculative looks at him, but Saul remained immune to the women who fancied themselves as a gunfighter's girl. He could never forget it had been a demure, golden haired schoolmarm who had nearly ended his career before it had begun with her pistol. The importance of his quest came before everything else. He was as dedicated as any knight of Arthur's Table who searched for the Holy Grail.

Now he believed he was getting closer to another of the five men he had sworn daily to his mother to destroy. Through his sources the Professor had learned the Cochise Kid had begun a career of highway robbery in the wild territory surrounding the little town of Conquest. Several times recently the Hobson Overland Company coach had been held up by a gang led by a man who fitted the description of the Cochise Kid. The thefts had been so serious the stage company faced ruin.

The Professor had gone ahead to Conquest to carry out a plan he had in mind.

'When you ride in say your name is Andrew Druce and you're an out-of-work cowboy,' he had instructed. 'I don't want the gang to find out that you're in town. Maybe it would be a good idea if you grew a beard. I'll contact you when you arrive.'

Saul, with a prickly reddish growth which contrasted with his long, almost white hair, had waited some days before taking the long ride that led north across the Old Spanish Trail into the empty lands bordering Utah. and He was in no hurry and his mount ambled contentedly along the track which curved between the gently waving clusters of bunch grass. As he rode, Saul watched with amusement the antics of a road runner, or chaparral bird, which moved beside the trail in a series of quick dashes as though challenging horse and rider to a race.

Suddenly the bird swerved away and began a strange, hopping dance by a patch of Spanish Dagger. The chilling sound of a rattlesnake floated to Saul's ears. Urging his reluctant mount off the trail, he rode over to watch the deadly duel which was now taking place. The rattler was swaying in anger and lunging at the bird whenever it came within range of its death-dealing fangs.

The road runner, one of the few creatures who has no fear of the whirring Lord of the Desert, fought by teasing the snake. It would flutter forward, dodge as the snake struck, and then, before it could draw back, peck its head. The infuriated reptile swayed on its coils, the loose joints in its trail 'rattling' angrily.

Again and again the comical bird hopped into the attack, and each time the snake's head came near it managed to make a dagger blow with its sharp little beak.

Soon the movements of the rattlesnake became slower. It had lost an eye and it began to slide over the sand towards the protection of the sharp, pointed leaves of the Spanish Dagger. The road runner swooped in front of it, flapping its wings in a frenzy to stop its escape.

Once more the bewildered rattler darted its head at the tantalising bird, and this time it lost the other eye. The long diamond-patterned body thrashed in agony, throwing up spurts of sand as it writhed hopelessly in a great circle. And at every opportunity the road runner fluttered forward and continued its remorseless pecking at the mutilated head.

At last the snake gave a convulsive shudder and lay still.

The bird began a funny dance of victory over its dead foe and Saul returned to the trail, reflecting that it was not only men who fought their duels to the death. There was something to be learned from the fight. The rattler was more deadly but the little road runner was more cunning and, above all, quicker.

It was noon when Saul saw the river ahead of him. It was broad and running fast with the extra water the warmth of spring had brought down from the distant, snow covered mountains. The trail went down to the bank, vanished below the glittering surface and reappeared on the other side.

Saul dismounted by an old, bullet pocked sign which said in crude letters: *Deadman's Ford – Beware if water reaches here*. The surface of the river was still a long way from the post. Bending down, he took off his boots and strung them round his neck. The Colt Frontier was placed inside his shirt. Back in the saddle he removed the Winchester from its sheath, and holding it high in his left hand, approached the ford.

The horse snorted in protest as the chill water swirled about it, but Saul patted its neck and encouraged it. Gradually the river deepened and as the middle was reached the surface was level with Saul's holster.

Saul kept his eyes on a group of willows opposite to check he and his horse were not being forced downstream by the current. Suddenly from the foliage there was a puff of smoke. With a neigh of terror the horse reared in the water, bloody foam frothing from its nostrils. Then it rolled sideways and as a second bullet threw up a fountain of spray close by, Saul just managed to gulp a deep breath before he found himself underwater. He released the hold on the nine pound rifle as the current whirled him away from the ford.

Luckily as a boy in Paradise Saul's happiest hours had been spent in the local swimming hole, and now his swimming ability saved him. Knowing the river curved round a bend a short distance from the ford, he fought to keep his head beneath the surface until he would be hidden from the unknown sniper.

At last he could no longer stand the agony of his bursting lungs. He raised his head and found the river had carried him out of sight of the willow clump.

Now he swam with the fast river until he was about a mile downstream from the ford. Here more willows grew on the opposite bank and he struggled across the current to them until he was able to grip their trailing branches. He was out of breath and his body was trembling with cold and he had to cling to the osiers for some minutes before he could summon up the strength to haul himself clear.

Cautiously climbing through the fringe of trees he found that the land stretched empty and flat to the distant outline of a mesa. Of the rifleman there was no sign. Saul hoped that he would think he had accomplished his murderous task, especially as he had not reappeared on the surface.

Still in the shelter of the trees he took the Colt out from his shirt and then undressed himself. He wrung the water form his clothes and then spread them out behind a low rock where they would be unlikely to attract attention. Then he went to work on the Colt, taking out the cartridges and drying it as best he could. Finally he stretched himself naked by his clothing and closed his eyes gratefully as the rays of the sun warmed his body.

An hour later he sat up and pulled on his shirt and Levis which were almost dry. His boots and holster were still wet, but on checking his gun he was relieved to find it was in working order. He made a mental note to oil it at the first opportunity.

He stood up and began to walk in the direction of the far mesa, knowing that sooner or later he would strike the trail that led to Conquest. At the moment he preferred to keep away from it in case he should run into another ambush.

Like most Westerners, Saul hated walking, especially in this loose, sandy soil in which his boots sank at every step. As he trudged he wondered why he had been shot at. Only the Professor knew he had been taking the Conquest trail, so that ruled out an assassin with a grudge. Perhaps it had been a bandit who had tried to kill him for whatever money he had in his pockets. Saul shrugged, bitter in the knowledge he had not seen the sniper, and even if he stood next to him in a bar someday he would not be able to recognise him and settle the score.

\* \* \*

The moon rose above the mesa and flooded the plain with ghostly light. The yi-yi-yip call of a distant coyote floated on the night wind. It died away to be replaced by the coughing roar of a cougar.

'I don't like them mountain lions,' said one of the two men sitting before a small fire close to the Conquest Trail. 'I once saw a fella that'd tangled with one.' He shivered.

'It's a long way off,' his companion said, throwing sage-brush branches on to the small blaze. 'Anyways, this'll keep it from comin' close. Cougars are plumb terrified of fire. How's the coffee comin'.

'Smells all right, Sebe,' was the reply. 'Say, what was that rustlin' in the sage?'

Both strained their ears.

'Guess it was the ponies,' said Sebe. 'One thing, it weren't no cougar. The ponies would've have gone plumb loco if one came close.'

'Hope you're right.'

' 'Course I'm right, Ed. Trouble is you're gettin' nervous.'

'Maybe. I just wish we knew for sure that crittur were killed this mornin'.

They say he's sudden death...'

'He *was* sudden death, you mean. I saw it clear as I see that fire. My first shot got his horse, I reckon I got him with the second bullet as it plunged. Anyway, whether I did or not, he went under the water an' he never surfaced. He's dead all right...'

'There is somethin' out there,' muttered Ed, glancing beyond the circle of firelight.

'Yeah, an' it ain't no cougar, either,' came a cool voice. 'Throw up your hands.'

'Like hell,' cried Sebe. He raised the rifle that had been lying across his knees and fired in the direction of the voice.

Ed drew his Colt and backed away from the fire.

'It's him,' he muttered. 'He's come back...'

'You're damn right,' floated the voice out of the sage.

Sebe fired again. The tethered ponies nearby whickered in terror at the shot.

From the shadowy sage there came the flash of a pistol and a curse from Sebe. Ed fired wildly at the gun flash with his revolver. Again the unseen gun exploded and a bullet cut a long furrow in the sand close to Sebe as he scrambled out of the glare of the flames. Once he was in the shadow he began returning the fire. Ed had meanwhile melted into the darkness in the direction of the plunging ponies.

With a warm trickle of blood soaking his shirt, Sebe crouched in the shadow of a stunted Joshua tree. Over his rifle he scanned the silver-lit sage beyond the flickering fire.

To his ears came the muffled thudding of hooves from the direction of the trail.

'Ed, you yellow-gutted son of a bitch!' he shouted in fury. His voice gave him away. There was the roar of a Colt Frontier and Sebe, the sniper of Deadman's Ford, pitched forward into eternity.

Into the firelight stepped Saul Powers, loading fresh cartridges into the Colt's cylinder. For a moment he looked down at the dark shape of Sebe, then turned to the camp-fire and poured himself out a mug of coffee. He had had his reckoning, but he still did not know why the late Sebe had tried to take his life.

# CHAPTER 10

Beneath the towering wall of the mesa stood a ramshackle building, across the front of which was the faded sign, 'Olsen's American Store.' It had been there for a dozen years, doing just enough trade with trail travellers and wandering Indians to support its whisky-loving owner, Pete Olsen, and his Kiowa wife whose Indian name meant 'Voice that runs like an eternal mountain cascade,' but which Pete had abbreviated to 'Big Mouth.'

It was into this humble emporium that Saul Powers stepped the morning after his battle with the mysterious Sebe. He found a mean-looking, shifty-eyed man behind the counter, a glass of rye close at hand in case of fainting spells, as he explained to his occasional customers.

When he saw Saul his eyes narrowed and he fortified himself with a quick gulp of the Old Vermont.

'Howdy, stranger,' he said. 'Lookin' for somethin'?'

'That's the size of it,' Saul replied, his eyes ranging over the meagre display of goods. 'I lost my hoss with all my gear on it.'

'At Deadman's Ford? Well, you ain't the first that's had to walk here to get fitted out again. What can I sell ya?'

'A beddin' roll, a rifle, a hoss an' a saddle,' said Saul.

'There's the beddin'.' Olsen pointed to some bundles in a corner. 'The rifles are in that rack. I got a couple trade hosses at the back.'

Saul walked over to the rifles, which had a chain through their trigger guards.

'Let's take a look at that Winchester,' he said.

'You ridin' on to Conquest?' asked Olsen while Saul examined the gun.

'Guess there ain't no other place to ride on to.'

'In that case you'll need extra water. You'll have to cross The Shimmer. I'll go an tell the wife to fill you a coupla skins.'

Half an hour later Saul resumed his journey on the best horse Olsen had to offer. There was a new rifle in his sheath and, as well as the canteen hanging from his Californian saddle, a leather water bag gurgled each side of his bedding roll.

As the mesa dwindled behind him Saul noticed a gradual change in the terrain. The ground was more rocky, the vegetation more sparse, the bunch grass giving way to clumps of prickly pear. By evening he reckoned he would reach the edge of the waterless wilderness which had to be crossed before he reached Conquest.

The whole of the western sky was aflame when he halted for the night and camped. Soon he had a can of beans cooking over a small fire while his horse rasped its tongue against the canvas bucket which had been filled from the canteen.

'Reckon that fella was right to sell me them two water skins,' Saul muttered to himself. 'I guess it's gonna be a thirsty day tomorrow.'

\* \* \*

The Shimmer had been rightly named. A vast expanse of broken rock, it offered neither shade not comfort to man or beast. An hour after sunrise the air began to dance above it so the horizon appeared as though seen through delirium.

The trail wound round outcrops of burning stone. Soon Saul had difficulty in following it, the only indication he was on the right path being an infrequent arrow painted on a rock by earlier travellers or cairns of rubble which had been erected long ago. Once drovers had attempted to drive a large herd across The Shimmer instead of circling it, and the white skulls of longhorns beside the track became Saul's most reliable guide.

He consoled himself he had plenty of water and by the end of the next day he should be clear of the desert and on the last leg of his journey. The sweat poured down his face and he rode with his bandana in his hand to wipe his eyes. Several times he unscrewed the cap of his canteen and raised it to his lips. The heat was so great that after each drink his shirt darkened with sweat, only to dry out again leaving white salt patches.

Once he pushed back his broad brimmed hat and gazed up at the brazen sky above. High above him a black dot hung as though suspended by an invisible wire. A buzzard.

By noon waves of heat reflected from the rock and smote the traveller like the blasts from an open furnace.

Saul halted the horse and swung wearily to the ground. He reached for the canteen but one shake assured him it was empty. He took down one of the water skins and filled the canvas bucket for his horse. The horse craned its neck down and sniffed at the water.

'Come on, ole gal,' said Saul. 'Don't be fussy about good water in this corner of hell.' Taking his tin mug he scooped it full from the bucket and gulped a mouthful, wincing at the bitter taste.

The tin fell with a clang to the rock, and the sun-blasted world began to spin before Saul's eyes.

'Drugged!' he muttered as the dark specks before his eyes converged into a spinning tunnel of darkness down which he was drawn.

The buzzard which had followed horse and rider through the morning plummeted down and perched on the skull of a long dead steer. The horse sniffed at the water again, snorted with disgust, and then slowly wandered away among the rocks.

Another buzzard settled, then another. Soon there was a patient circle round the sprawled figure.

* * *

Shadows began to lengthen from the millions of rocks which made up the face of The Shimmer. The circle of buzzards round Saul Powers began to flutter their wings and shake their obscene bald heads with impatience. Through the heat of the afternoon they had waited for the moment of death and the feast it would herald, but the hoarse breathing of their prey had continued. Luckily for Saul he had fallen forward so his hat gave protection to his neck and head.

Now as The Shimmer cooled, and the rock cracked as it contracted, he opened his eyes, escaping from a nightmare in which he had been fighting a slow motion battle with a gigantic rattlesnake.

For a moment there was a feeling of relief of having escaped from the horrible dream, then his eyes focused on the birds watching with pitiless eyes. He moved his head painfully, and the birds croaked with consternation.

'Til give you somethin' to croak about,' he muttered. Slowly raising himself to a sitting position, he put his hand down to the Frontier strapped low on his thigh. As his fingers closed on the smooth bone of the butt a sense of relief flooded through him – he was still alive, and what was more he was still armed. He'd give those damn birds a run for their money yet. He raised the gun and squeezed the sensitive trigger. The report was followed by a cloud of feathers and a noisy beating of wings.

For a moment the birds hovered, then Saul watched with disgust as several swooped down and savagely tore at the bird he had shot. There was something so alien about the birds' greed that he fired again and again until his gun was empty and the echo of his shots was rolled across the wilderness like strange thunder.

Having vented his hate on the buzzards, he slowly climbed to his feet, the smoking Colt hanging down in his left hand. As his mind cleared from the effects of the drugged sleep he began to take stock of his situation.

His horse had wandered off, he was without food or water, and he reckoned he was somewhere in the centre of The Shimmer. If he was to survive he had to get out of this barren wasteland by the next day – an impossible task. Yet there was nothing else for it, he would have to make the journey by foot.

The problem he would have to resolve would be whether to venture forward, or follow the trail back? He decided to go on. First, he had an inbred dislike of retracing his path, and secondly, if he went back he felt he would be likely to run into the forces which had twice planned his destruction. And he knew with a grim certainty that by the time he was clear of The Shimmer he would be in no condition to face his enemies.

He looked round the spot where he had lain so long in drugged stupor. Strangely enough, apart from a headache, he did not feel as bad as he would have expected. Perhaps he had not drunk enough of the water for it to have affected him badly. Maybe Big Mouth had not done her work well. Certainly the storekeeper had planned his death out there in The Shimmer by doping him, but it had misfired. Saul thought the drug was the same as he'd heard of used in West Coast ports to shanghai crews for Pacific whalers, or for fleecing greenhorns in shady gambling halls.

The bucket lay at his feet. The water had evaporated during the long afternoon. Saul kicked it away from him and began to march. On his left the sun died and a strange mauve light filled the vastness of The Shimmer, gradually darkening as the cool night approached.

He rested when the night became too black to make out the trail, waiting for the moonrise which he knew would illuminate the landscape well enough for him to travel. With his back to a rock that still held some warmth from the day, he sat and listened to the strange sighing sounds whispered through the darkness. No wonder the Indians avoided the area believing it was a meeting place of spirits.

As a silver radiance began to spread across the sky Saul hauled himself to his feet, glad to be moving on once more. Like all deserts, a characteristic of The Shimmer was that while it was a hell on earth during the day, its temperature dropped dramatically during the night.

The trail stretched ahead endlessly, marked by stones and skulls. The surface was so rough that sometimes Saul tripped on rock fragments, bruising himself badly. Sometimes he whistled, hoping that by some chance his mount had strayed in this direction. But the only reply was the eerie soughing of a night breeze moving in phantom gusts across the face of The Shimmer. After a while Saul stopped whistling. His mouth, which had a bitter taste in it after the knockout drug, was getting dry and he could no longer purse his dry lips.

As he continued his march memories began to haunt him. First, there was the vivid picture of his father lying in the yard with the five killers sitting on their horses coolly emptying their guns into his body. Then he was a child again, striving to remember his 'promise' correctly. The names floated through his mind: 'Lew O'Hara...Ben Rockwell...Charlie Gideon...Jesse Nathan...The CochiseKid.'

The memories came closer to the present. Again he saw Lew O'Hara fall on Silver Street; again he saw the terrible dying face of Charlie Gideon in the lurid light of his gun-flashes. So far he had kept faith with his 'promise.' Now the Cochise Kid was waiting at the end of his journey, unaware of Nemesis marching across the moonlit wilderness.

'I've gotta live, I've gotta live,' Saul muttered, forcing his weary limbs to move faster. 'There ain't no sense in it if I cash in now.'

The strange moan of The Shimmer was his only reply.

\* \* \*

The dawn brought new life to Saul. Again he had rested during the hours of utter darkness, but now as rosy light flooded the east he got painfully to his feet. Looking down at his boots he saw the sharp rock had damaged them badly. He wondered if they would last him through the day. He had debated as to whether to rest through the heat. Perhaps he could find a rock under which he could crouch until evening, but already thirst was beginning to .torture him and he decided to move on for as long as he could.

For a brief time The Shimmer was a place of desolate beauty. It was still cool, and strange colours glowed in the rocks and veins of quartz sparkled. But by the time Saul had managed to cover a couple of miles the horizon had begun its familiar dance, and the sweat was trickling down his face.

He walked with his head bowed, his eyes almost hypnotised by the sight of his feet moving over the trail. A strange chant began to hammer in his mind: 'Right foot...left foot...right foot...left foot...'

Every so often he would shake his head and look around to break the spell and check he was still on the trail. His body ached with fatigue. He had heard tell how men in his position jettisoned their belongings as they weakened, first, their empty water bottles, then their ammunition, then money, finally their guns...Well, he'd be damned if he'd do that. His gun and ammunition belt was all that he carried so there was no chance of lightening the load. But by mid-morning he found his hands fumbling at the buckle of his heavy gun belt. He took it off and removed a dozen cartridges. These he put in his pocket. He drew out the Frontier and thrust it in his waistband, then threw the belt and the remaining shells down on the trail. For a while he felt better without the familiar weight. Then his head bowed again and the familiar 'Left foot...right foot...left foot' returned to beat in his brain.

Sometimes his smarting eyes scanned the ground about him, searching for a sign of vegetation which would hint he was nearing the end of The Shimmer, or maybe a barrel cactus which was said to contain water in the pulp within its tough, spiked rind. But there was nothing...nothing except the rock and the eye-searing glitter of mica patches.

*Right foot... left foot... right foot...*

Panic hit Saul when he found himself lying face down on the trail. He had not remembered falling. He had just passed out on his feet and the pain of the fall had jerked him back to awareness.

There was a great temptation to lay there and rest – just for a little while – but he knew the danger of this. Checking the Colt Frontier was still safely in his waistband, he staggered up and recommenced his march.

The shadows at the base of the rocks told him noon approached. Above the sun was like a huge ball of fire. In his fevered imagination so close he could almost feel the savage lick of the flames.

A cackle of laughter burst through his cracked lips.

'Goddam it,' he cried aloud. 'First, I nearly freeze to death in the river, an' now...' He laughed again, and an echo of his laughter made him turn drunkenly.

'Who the hell is laughin' in this place?' he demanded.

Now as he trudged he spoke to himself at frequent intervals. The curse of the desert was taking its toll. Delirium was waiting for him in the quivering heat waves. When he looked up from his scuffed and broken boots a mirage danced ahead – a mirage of glittering water fringed with green trees, reminding him of somewhere he had been recently.

At last his knees buckled under him again.

'Must rest, must rest,' he gasped and he heaved himself into the slender shadow of a rock. For a few moments he closed his eyes. When he opened them he saw crude writing scratched on a boulder half-buried in sand opposite him.

*HERE LIES*
*JACK ROSCOE*
*BURIED BY HIS PARD*

Saul hoisted his tortured body up and once more he began to stagger forward. His mind had cleared briefly and his thoughts were filled with the forgotten tragedy commemorated by those few words.

He wondered what sort of a man Jack Roscoe had been, and he wondered at the calibre of his partner who had painfully chipped his epitaph.

Time passed, but its passing lost all meaning for Saul. His nerves were taut with pain, his mouth and throat were burning and to his horror he realised his tongue was starting to protrude from his lips. The next time he fell he was unable to get back on his feet. Instead he began crawling forward on his hands and knees. No longer had he any sense of direction, only a blind urge to go on.

He began to move off the trail, but came to an abrupt halt, face to face with a skull which looked up at him ironically from a patch of sand. Perhaps it was Jack Roscoe's 'pard'.

Saul knew he could go no farther. He rolled over into the shade and drew his Colt. He raised the muzzle to his lips with a vague recollection that the sucking of metal can assuage thirst. But the gun was hot and there was no saliva left in his mouth, and he dropped it beside the silent, grinning skull.

* * *

At sundown he revived and managed to get back on the track, continuing his journey in a series of staggering lurches. Again the mauve settled over The Shimmer and a cool breeze wafted against his bearded face. He looked about him, and saw by the trail a withered clump of mesquite. Farther on there was a ragged growth of prickly pear. Obviously he was nearing the limit of The Shimmer, but how much farther would he have to go before he found a well or creek.

Yet the fact that he had almost crossed the wilderness lent him new strength and he pressed on to find the rock giving way to drifts of sand covered with patches of chaparral.

Ahead he thought he saw a light. At first he dismissed it as some illusionary Jack o' Lantern, but it remained even after he had turned his head and rubbed his eyes. As he got closer to the beacon he fancied he heard something that took him back to a childhood time in a mission hall in Paradise. At first he could not believe it, and then there was no doubt. It was an accordion playing *Shall We Gather At the River*.

# CHAPTER 11

In the glow of the fire Saul saw that the wagon was an old style 'Conestoga.' Painted on its white canvas cover in letters of brilliant scarlet was the word 'REPENT', and beneath it was the legend, *The Wages of Sin is Death*. As Saul reeled forward the accordion music stopped and a tall man with a silvery mane of hair ran forward to catch him.

'Rachel, Rachel!' he called. 'Bring water quick, there's a poor sufferer come to us from The Shimmer.'

Gently he laid Saul down on a blanket, and then Saul was aware of a girl bending over him, moistening his lips with a handkerchief she soaked from a canteen.

Roughly he pulled the canteen from her and thrusting the neck into his mouth, gulped spasmodically until it was empty. Then he laid it to one side with a moan of satisfaction.

'Take it easy, son,' said the man. 'I guess you must have been pretty parched, but you gotta take things kinda gradual.'

'I beg pardon,' muttered Saul to the girl. 'I guess I was plumb crazy for water. Is there some more, please?'

'In a moment,' she said quietly, and leaning forward she began wiping his face with the handkerchief. Looking up at her Saul was aware of a calm oval face framed by long, gleaming black hair which fell in two strands almost to her waist. In the flickering shadows of the dancing fire it was impossible to tell the colour of her eyes, but he was later to see that they were a deep violet shade. After the horror of the day she appeared like a vision.

'I guess that water was real, but you – everythin' else could be a mirage,' he murmured. She smiled, her generous mouth curving into a slow sensitive smile revealing strong, even teeth.

'Guess we're real enough,' she said softly. 'Lucky we are for your sake, stranger, the nearest water hole is ten miles off. What's your name?'

'Andrew... Andrew Druce. I was crossin' The Shimmer an'...'

'Save it, son,' said the man. 'You can tell us all about it after you've rested some. Rachel, get some blankets to put over him, an' help me get them boots offa his feet. I can guess they must be in a pretty bad shape.'

A strange dreamy peace filled Saul while the man and girl tended to him. She washed the blood from the places where he had gashed himself when he had fallen on the trail. She rubbed a salve on to the parts of his flesh which had been exposed to the sun and were a mass of painful blisters. He did not stir from his trance as his rags were taken off him and he was dressed in a clean linen shirt and cotton trousers. Only when the girl picked up the Colt Frontier he muttered inaudibly through the sleep that was engulfing him.

She looked at the revolver with distaste, then, seeing his face, put it down beside him. He stretched out his hand and grasped the bone butt. Then his eyes closed and he began to sleep with a smile on his face.

He was awakened by Rachel.

'Breakfast,' she said. 'I've made you come gruel...'

'Gruel,' cried Saul. 'Lady, you ain't by any chance got some bacon an' eggs an' maybe some canned tomatoes an'...'

She laughed.

'Easy on, stranger. You nearly died of thirst

yesterday, remember? That isn't very good for your insides, and you must take things slowly. Maybe if you behave yourself you can have something more substantial later on, maybe for supper. But I'm not going to make you sick just as you are starting to get better. Why, last night I thought you'd burst yourself the way you took down that water.'

Saul grinned at her.

'Guess I musta seemed pretty wild an' ornery.' He pushed back the blankets to sit up and noticed he was in clean clothes.

'Saaay,' he began awkwardly, 'Was it you who...'

She nodded. 'Don't fret about it,' she laughed. Saul, red faced, said nothing.

'You didn't seem to mind last night,' she added. 'Only thing that bothered you was when I tried to take your gun away.'

'I guess I'm usta havin' it around. May I ask your names so I can thank you proper?'

'I am Rachel Prescott. My father is the Reverend Elijah Prescott. Everyone calls him Padre, so do I.'

'Well, Miss Prescott, I wanna thank...'

'I know,' she said. 'I am thankful we were here when you were in need.'

'The work of the Lord,' declared the Reverend Prescott coming up. 'It was only by accident we were here. One of the horses had gone lame and I stopped to rest it up. Now, son, have your gruel an' then we'll talk.'

'I'll go make coffee,' said Rachel. She rose to her feet and Saul caught his breath at the sight of her supple young figure silhouetted against the early morning sky. She was wearing a white blouse with a collar high up her throat and a skirt of a pale grey material which reached the ground, but these garments could not hide the exciting contours of her body nor the natural grace of her movement. As she stood, smiling at him, the light breeze blew a strand of hair across her finely cut features and Saul realised he had never seen a girl of such beauty before.

'Eat your gruel while it's warm,' she laughed, and turning she went to the rear of the Conestoga from where a mouth-watering smell of coffee soon wafted.

'Now tell us, son, what happened to you out there?' said the Padre when the three had steaming tin mugs in their hands.

'I was half way across The Shimmer when I had an accident,' said Saul. 'I lost my cayuse an' I had to come the rest of the way on my feet.'

'It's a miracle,' said the tall preacher. 'I didn't think anyone could have survived The Shimmer. Folks say the Devil put it there to let the world know what hell'd be like.'

'I guess I wouldn't have made it if it hadn't been for you an' your daughter. Had you come across?'

'Never. I was just skirting the northern limit on my way to do the work of the Lord. As you see I'm a travellin' preacher. My home – an' my daughter's – is this wagon. It has been since her dear mother went to her rest long ago. I go from place to place, sayin' the Word, maybe givin' a little comfort when I can, tryin' to save a few souls. There's plenty need a-savin'. But don't you worry none. I ain't gonna try an' convert you while you ain't in no position to duck,' and he laughed richly.

'Maybe Mister – er – Druce don't need saving,' said Rachel. 'He's got an honest face under that beard I'll be bound.'

'Where are you headin' for, son?' asked the Padre.

'Conquest,' said Saul. 'Lookin' for work.'

'Well, that's the direction we are goin'. I'd reckoned to preach the Word there this comin' Sabbath.

From what I hear, Conquest could use a bit of honest hellfirin'. I hope you'll come with us.'

'That's mighty kind. I guess I just don't know how to thank you both.'

'You're welcome. How could I preach about the Good Samaritan if I didn't put my money where my mouth is.'

'Tell me, Mister Druce, when you were asleep last night you were talking some,' said Rachel, suddenly looking Saul in the eye. 'You were saying something about poisoned water. Had someone poisoned your water? And you kept repeating the names of five men. I can't remember them, and it isn't my business...but one was the Cochise Kid. Now I do believe he is some sort of law-breaker who has been causing trouble round Conquest.'

'I guess you talk a lot of nonsense when you've been sick with the sun,' said Saul. 'I hope I didn't keep you awake, Miss Rachel.'

She looked at him gravely. 'Time for me to put some more oil on those blisters.' As she dressed his right arm she said: 'That's a strange scar you have. It just looks like a gunshot wound. You have been in the wars, Mister – uh – Druce.'

\* \* \*

The next day the old covered wagon rolled along the trail towards Conquest. To Saul, rested after his ordeal and conscious of the warm personality of Rachel Prescott, it was a journey of delight. As the heavy horses plodded on the Padre joked and played his accordion to pass the time, and Rachel sang the old hymn tunes in a clear voice. Saul had never heard hymns sung like that before and he was amazed that a preacher and his daughter could be such fun.

'I always thought padres – if you'll excuse me sayin' so – were always on about sin an' the Demon Rum an' all,' he said.

'Don't you worry about that,' said Rachel. 'If you come to a meeting you'll hear all about sin. The Padre is one of the most hellfiringest preachers west of the Great Divide. I've seen tough gunmen break into tears of remorse when he gets going. Talking about that, have you ever known any gunfighters, Mister Druce?'

'I seen some, I reckon,' said Saul carelessly. 'They don't interest me none.'

'I'm glad,' Rachel said. 'I believed the most evil thing of the West is the so called gunfighter. The fact that some misguided fools think of him as some sort of a hero just shows how much people have gone astray in their thinking. How can anyone have a respect for a man who lives just for the purpose of killing his fellow beings? What glory is there in his sordid killings – his senseless wanderings in search of fresh victims just to satisfy some warped vanity.

'I'm sorry. I get carried away with anger when I think of it. Look at this magazine. A writer had written about some blood-lusting ruffian as though he was someone worthy of our admiration instead of a murderer who will probably end up on the gallows.'

Into Saul's hand she thrust an old copy of the *Frontier Journal*, which, despite its name, was published in New York.

'Now just read that,' she said. The article on page five.'

Saul opened the magazine and found the place.

He gave a start. Under banner headlines was an article about him. The heading said:

### Boy Gunfighter Blazes Vengeance Trail.

Under it was the byline of Jonathan Coffin. Slowly he read the opening:

*With blazing six-guns, Saul Powers, son of Luke Powers the famous gunfighter, is riding a vengeance trail across the western half of the continent to slay the men who foully murdered his father twelve years ago.*

*Dedicated to his trusty revolver, young Powers is said to have inherited his father's skill with the 'hardware from Hartford' and then some. This was demonstrated recently when he caught up with one of the gang in the town of Gila Springs. Here, before the amazed citizens, he fought a battle to the death with saloon-owner Lew O'Hara himself a man noted for his prowess with a pistol and with many successful handgun engagements behind him.*

*It was around nine in the morning when Saul Powers began his slow walk up Silver Street, a walk that was to end in death for O'Hara when the youth's special white-handled Colt leapt into blazing action...*

The story continued for several pages, and there was an artist's impression of the gunfight. It showed Saul with a gun in each hand, firing simultaneously.

'Seems a crazy story to me,' said Saul with an attempt at casualness, handing back the magazine. 'These things get pretty fantastic when they're written in the papers. Why, I'll bet the fella who wrote that was never within a hundred miles of Gila Springs. These journalist guys make most of it up, just for the money.'

'You might be right,' said Rachel, taking back the magazine. 'I just pray and look forward to the day when the West is peaceful and prosperous and god-fearing.'

'Amen to that,' agreed Saul piously, though his mind was in a strange confusion at having read this account of himself.

'Let's change the subject anyway,' Rachel said. 'It depresses me so much to even think about it...by the way, Mister Druce, that's a very expensive looking pistol you have...'

* * *

Saul said goodbye to his friends at Conquest.

'Do come to the meetin' on Sunday,' said the Padre. 'It's always good to see a friendly face in the crowd.'

'I'll sure do that if I can,' said Saul.

'Please remember,' added Rachel quietly. 'It would be a pity if we did not meet again. Meanwhile, good luck, Mister Druce.'

The old Conestoga creaked down the street and Saul entered the hall of Kelly's Rooming House. Having registered himself as Andrew Druce, he went and lay on his bed. There were two things on his mind. The first was Rachel Prescott and secondly, and much less importantly, the story of the vengeance trail which had no doubt entertained thousands of magazine readers back East.

But he did not have long with his thoughts. There was a knock on the door and Kelly handed him a note.

'It jest came for you, Mister Druce, it did,' he explained. 'Sure, a body don't have to be in Conquest long before all the world knows he's here. I sure hope it's good news you'll be reading.'

Gently closing the door, Saul opened the note.

*Come at dusk to the Hobson Overland Company—J.C. Prof. Eng. Lit.*

The rest of the afternoon Saul spent taking the Colt Frontier to pieces and oiling it. When the trigger mechanism worked to his satisfaction and the cylinder spun true and free he began practising in front of the fly-spotted mirror. He found the new gunbelt he had purchased a little awkward at first, but after greasing the holster and trimming it with his pocket knife he began to feel more confident.

Soon after sundown he stepped out into the street and made his way unobtrusively to the office of the stage company. As soon as he knocked on the glass panelled door he was admitted, to find the Professor and a stout, smiling man behind a desk with a bottle of whisky before him.

'Welcome,' said the Professor. 'Meet Marty Hobson, owner of the Hobson Overland Company.'

Saul shook hands.

'Have a shot,' invited the genial Hobson.

Saul nodded.

'Have a good journey?' continued Hobson, pouring out a generous drink.

'Not bad,' said Saul. The Shimmer was a bit hot.'

Marty Hobson nodded.

'Well, son, the Professor here has told me all about you, an' let me say here and now how mighty glad an' relieved I am that you've come. Four times my coach has been held up in the last two months. Not only were the passengers skinned right out, but twice it was carryin' bullion. Confidence in my outfit has dropped to zero, an' if it happens again I guess I could be out of business. Now, look at this map an' I'll show you where it happened...'

'How did the road agents work?' Saul asked.

'It varied. Once it was a tree across the trail. Once the coach came round a bend an' there were three masked men waiting for it with rifles. The shotgun tried to make a fight, but they blasted him down. Poor Johnny.'

For a moment the good humour left Hobson's face and he looked strained and serious.

'I think there is no doubt that it is the Cochise Kid,' said the Professor. 'Do you remember what he looks like, Saul?'

'I reckon so.'

'Maybe this will refresh your memory,' and from his pocket the Professor took his leather-covered notebook out of which he took a folded broadsheet. It had the picture of a gaunt-looking man with high cheekbones and large ears. Beneath it was printed a long list of his crimes.

'I know him all right,' said Saul. 'The only difference between that picture and what I remember is that when he gunned down my father he was smilin'.'

# CHAPTER 12

Saul took his place in the coach as it stood outside the Hobson Overland Company. In the corner sat the Professor, enigmatic as usual behind his tinted spectacles. He took no notice of Saul and, for his part, Saul ignored him as they had arranged the night before.

A well-stocked bullion box was heaved aboard by three sweating bank clerks. The shotgun guard clambered on to the roof, the driver cracked his long rawhide. The stage rolled down the main street of Conquest to the barking of a number of dogs who raced beside the large wheels until the last of the buildings fell away and the coach was lurching along the northern trail.

Now Saul had a chance to examine his fellow passengers. Sitting opposite him was a small businessman, nervously puffing at a large cigar, and clasping a briefcase as though he expected it to be snatched away at any second. Next to him was a large man in a shabby frock-coat who had already taken a flat bottle from his pocket, while in the far corner was a cowboy, his saddle beneath the seat. On one side of Saul sat a sober-suited drummer, his sample bag on his lap. On the other side, and in the opposite corner to the Professor, sat a statuesque lady in a pink and lilac outfit. Her face was artfully made up and her perfume was so strong that it drowned the smell of whisky from the man in the frock-coat. When the travellers began to talk she announced that she was Arabella Love, a singer who was on tour, having performed at all the 'swell theatres back East.'

'Thas ri',' agreed the man with the bottle. 'I saw you las' ni' in Crystal Palace. Say, I laughed like hell when you kicked that fella's derby. Thish lil lady sure ish a high kicker, boys,' he said, turning to the rest of the coach. 'You jus' hang on to your hatsh if she gets started. Here, lesh drink to Mish Arabella Love an' her high kicksh. Have a swig, friend.'

He proffered the bottle to the businessman who shook his head with embarrassment.

'No thank you, sir,' he said primly. 'It is not my habit to touch strong waters.'

The drunk let out a great whisky-tainted guffaw.

'Thish ain't strong waters, friend,' he observed. 'This is strong goddam rotgut rye.' Chuckling at his wit, he proceeded to sample more.

'I do hope this will be a safe journey,' remarked Miss Arabella Love. 'I have heard that this stage has been held up by ruffians several times recently. It's all right for you men, you only lose your wallets, but a girl has much more at stake.'

'Don't worry on it, ma'am,' said the cowboy. 'There's a mighty good guard up there with the driver, an' if the Cochise Kid did turn up, waal, I'd see you come to no harm.'

Miss Love threw him a smile of gratitude from her exquisitely painted eyes. 'You make me feel so much safer...'

'Aw shucks, ma'am...'

The effect was spoiled by the patron of the Crystal Palace.

'If the Cochise Kid held us up, she kick the gunsh outa hish hands,' he announced. 'You should shee her legsh, boys...'

'That ain't no way to talk in front of a lady,' said the cowboy.

'I agree,' said the little businessman. 'It was most

indelicate. Don't you agree, sir?'

The remark was addressed to Saul.

'Uh? Oh sure, it's a wonder that Miss Arabella ain't gone down with the vapours,' he grinned. 'Maybe we had better change the subject before we all gets embarrassed.'

'I agree, I agree,' said the businessman. 'Tell me, sir, you are a commercial traveller. What is your line?'

'Firearms,' said the drummer briefly. 'Can I sell you a buffalo gun?'

After twenty miles of the journey the coach halted at a changing post. 'Five minutes for a drink,' called the driver. Saul grinned, remembering his experience when he had been a raw kid on his first journey from Paradise.

'Gimme a beer,' he ordered the barman in the small refreshment cabin. 'An' gimme my change first.'

The cowboy had been given gracious permission to buy Miss Arabella Love a large brandy, 'So good for the throat of an artiste when travelling,' and the man in the frock-coat managed to replenish his supply of rye.

So the morning passed. The positions of the travellers changed in the coach, the cowboy arranging to sit beside Miss Love so the firearms traveller sat opposite Saul. The drunk had grabbed the corner seat and there he contemplated his bottle and entertained himself with snatches of song.

Suddenly the swaying coach began to slow down. There was a cry and then the roar of a shotgun followed by a crackle of rifle fire.

'My Lord, a hold-up,' cried the businessman, his face the colour of clay.

'Take my jewels but leave me my honour!' screamed Arabella Love.

'Hands up, Powers,' said the arms salesman, and from his sample case, which he had open on his knee, he produced a .38 Police Colt. 'Go on, get them up – an' all the rest of you.'

Grimly Saul obeyed. Outside the rifle fire had died down, but someone was groaning in mortal agony. The .38 pointed unwaveringly at Saul's heart.

'You inside, come out an' don't try to be heroes,' came a harsh voice. 'You got Powers covered, Tom?'

'Sure have.'

The passengers climbed out to see three masked men sitting on horses, rifles pointed at the coach. On the box the driver sat like a statue, his hands high in the air. Beside him was slumped the guard, the blood from his wounds trickling down the side of the coach.

The man with the .38 lined the passengers one side of the trail while two of the hold-up men dismounted and entered the coach to get the bullion box.

'Now folks, shell out,' ordered the bandit who remained on the horse. 'Don't hold back or we'll strip you down.' (A scream from Miss Love). 'But you, Powers, an' your pal from the Press – keep your hands high. I know you got a pistol on you.'

'I think you have made some mistake about our identity,' said the Professor. 'This young man I happen to know is Andrew Druce...'

'Save your wind, fella. Hurry up with that cash box, boys.'

The passengers reluctantly presented their belongings to the bogus drummer who put them in a cloth bag which he had drawn from his sample case.

That all?' he demanded of the small businessman.

'I swear...'

Roughly he thrust his hand inside his coat. It reappeared with a flat packet of notes.

'I must have overlooked...'

The Police Colt swept in a sudden arc. The barrel

struck the little man on the temple and he sagged to the ground.

'Let that be a warnin',' shouted the mounted man. Saul saw that, though the bandana hid his features from the eyes down, he had large batwing ears. He was sure it was his sworn enemy.

From the creaking coach the other two masked men appeared struggling with the heavy box.

'It's sure a weight,' grunted one. 'Come on, cowboy, you can give us a hand with it...'

'Aw shucks,' said the young puncher.

'Don't leave me,' Miss Arabella Love implored.

'Guess I got to, ma'am. They got the drop on us.'

'That's right,' said the Cochise Kid. 'Just do as you're told an' in a few minutes you'll be on your way. All except you, Powers, an' your blue-glassed pal. We got somethin' sorta special for you. I hear tell you've been lookin' for me. Waal, you've come to the end of the search.' He laughed.

Saul, his arms aching, looked along the line of passengers. The drunk was hardly aware of what was happening. He had happily handed over his wallet but he had clung to his bottle with alcoholic determination. The businessman lay on the ground unconscious. The Professor seemed unruffled. There was a slight frown on his flabby features but nothing else.

'Okay, back into the coach,' ordered the Cochise Kid. For a moment the drummer looked away from Saul as the passengers moved forward. It was the chance he had been waiting for. His foot lashed out, the toe of his boot catching the man agonisingly on the knee-cap.

He toppled over with a curse and Saul thrust his hand inside his coat to where the Frontier was concealed. As he did so the fallen man raised the Police Colt. Before he could fire there was a high-pitched report and he fell back.

Meanwhile the two men who had been carrying the box with the aid of the cowboy dropped the heavy load, swung round with their guns and opened fire. The drunk gave a yelp of indignation as a bullet smashed the bottle in his hand.

Saul pulled the Frontier free and throwing it up to arms length, fired at the Cochise Kid. The bullet hit the bandit's horse, causing it to plunge wildly. Saul swung the sights round and fired again. One of the masked men toppled forward. The other began backing to cover. Saul sprang forward and crouched by the stage.

As he did he saw the Cochise Kid leap down from his unmanageable mount. In the shadow of the coach Saul raised his gun again and sent a couple of .44-.40 slugs crashing in the direction of the remaining road agents.

The Cochise Kid dived for cover behind the tree which had been dragged across the road to halt the stage. From here he blazed away at the coach, while his companion began a wide circle through the scrub which grew on each side of the trail with the idea of taking Saul from behind.

Saul was aware of a figure beside him. The driver had swung down from the coach and was standing behind him, the guard's bloodied shotgun in his hands.

'Good work, fella,' he hissed. 'We'll make those sons of bitches pray for what they did to my mate.'

'Watch out for that fella in the scrub,' said Saul. I'm goin' after Cochise...'

There was a roar of the shotgun close to his ear as the driver opened up.

Pausing to push new shells in his chambers with practised speed, Saul sprinted from the coach and threw himself into a narrow depression by the side of the trail. Now he had as much cover as the Cochise Kid. He only hoped that the driver would be able to keep the other outlaw occupied,

A bullet hit the earth close to him, throwing a spray of soil into his face.

Saul wiped his eyes with his left hand, then swung the sights on to the fallen tree. The smoke of the Cochise Kid's powder drifted lazily above it. Saul waited. Somewhere behind him there was another shotgun blast, then a quick burst of revolver shooting followed by a muffled curse of pain.

Over the barrel of the Frontier, Saul saw a gun above the tree trunk, then the top of a head. For a second he held his breath, then squeezed the trigger.

His bullet cut a gash in the top side of the trunk, but he could not see if it had caught the Cochise Kid.

Some instinct warned him of danger.

He looked up to see the other gunman nearby, calmly aiming at him. Without thinking Saul rolled over as the gun exploded. Before the man could shoot again Saul fired from his prone position. At this moment the hard tuition of Cole Allard, when he made Saul use his gun from every conceivable position, paid its dividend. The outlaw dropped his gun and clawed at the spreading patch of crimson below his right breast.

Saul turned back to the log, ready to fire again the instant the Cochise Kid should reappear. Nothing stirred. Saul began to move warily forward. Still no movement. Closer yet, then he leapt to his feet, firing at the figure lying behind the natural barricade. His bullets thudded into a corpse. Saul's earlier shot had not only grooved the bark of the tree, it had dispatched the desperado known as the Cochise Kid.

With the Colt still smoking Saul surveyed the scene of the battle. The bodies of the three coach robbers were strewn grotesquely on the trail, the other was now leaning back against the coach trying to staunch the flow of blood from his chest. The driver, still with the shotgun in his hand, lay where he had collapsed when a couple of revolver slugs had ripped into his thigh.

The rest of the passengers were picking themselves from the ground where they had thrown themselves during the swift gunfight. Saul saw the Professor slip something into his pocket.

'It was you!' he cried. 'You got that fella in the black suit just as he was aimin' at me!'

The Professor nodded and showed Saul the small derringer in his hand.

'I don't usually carry arms, as you know,' he said. 'But this time I thought an extra gun might be useful.' He smiled bleakly. 'That is the first time I have shot anybody. It feels rather curious.'

The bodies of the outlaws were laid out by the trail and the tree trunk was dragged to one side. Then, with the bullion box back in the coach and the wounded men laid out as comfortably as possible, the cowboy flicked the reins and the team strained at the harness. Splattered with blood and showing several bullet holes, the coach caused a sensation when it reached Holtsville.

\* \* \*

'I must go to the telegraphic office,' said the Professor when the Holtsville marshal had taken charge of the Hobson Overland stage.

'It should make a good story,' said Saul with irony.

'I am sure it will,' replied the Professor. 'But on this occasion I am expecting a telegraphic message. Come with me, you may find it of interest.'

At the small office he gave his name and was handed a roughly printed message. It said: CONFIRM WELLS FARGO PLAN OPERATION HOLTSVILLE-CONQUEST SERVICE.

'You see what that means,' said the Professor.

'Marty Hobson was in league with the Cochise Kid. Knowing he was going to be forced out of business, he had his own coach robbed. I began to suspect something when you told me of your adventures on the Conquest Trail. No one except Hobson knew that you were coming. Obviously your safe arrival was the last thing he wanted, so he fixed to have you killed off. And then when he knew you'd be riding in the stage to trap Cochise he planned to have a member of the gang sitting opposite you.',

'It all figures,' said Saul. 'I reckon he ain't gonna be too pleased when we walk into his office.'

'You could be right,' said the Professor. 'Last night I telegraphed a man I know in the Wells Fargo office, instructing him to wire me here. I also took the precaution of buying a gun.'

'Let's see if the marshal can rustle up a couple of bosses,' said Saul. 'I'm rather anxious to get back to Conquest.'

It was Sunday morning when Saul and the Professor, covered with trail dust, swung down from their saddles and walked across the wooden walk to the office of the Hobson Overland Company.

'Sure hope he's here/ murmured Saul, pushing through the door.

'Why...howdy boys,' came the genial voice of the stage line owner, but the usual smile on his face had turned to a frozen grimace as he sat at his desk.

'Howdy, Mister Hobson,' said Saul.

'You got through all right...'

'Had a mighty fine trip, thanks...'

Hobson suddenly made a rapid movement. A gun appeared in his hand from the secret hiding place in the desk. But before he could fire Saul's hand flashed down to his holster to reappear with the Frontier. The bullet shattered the bone of Hobson's arm and his gun thudded to the floor unused.

With a groan he slumped back in his chair.

'All right, boys, you win,' he gasped. 'I got all that bullion stashed away...I'll split it with you...you can have two-thirds, how about that...come on, boys, give me a break...you can have the whole goddam lot...'

Saul looked down at him with contempt. 'Get you to your feet,' he snapped. 'We're gonna take a walk to the marshal's office.'

\* \* \*

A large tent had been erected on the outskirts of Conquest. Close by it stood an old covered wagon with the word 'REPENT' painted on its side. From inside the tent came the sound of accordion music and voices joining in a rousing hymn. Next to the spectacle of a gun fight, there was nothing the honest citizens of Conquest enjoyed more than a real red-hot Gospeller.

The singing ended, and Saul could hear the voice of the Padre ringing out loud and clear.

'People of Conquest,' he said. 'I've come to save your sinful souls...' There were some ironical cheers and a couple of 'Hallelujahs.'

Saul slipped inside the entrance and saw his friend standing up like some old prophet behind a portable pulpit.

'I know there's sinners here in this town,' thundered the preacher happily. There's those that drink...there's those that swear...there are those of you who play games of chance, and there are those who lust after scarlet women; and even worse—there are those who regard the Colt as their god...'

As Saul watched he was conscious of someone close to him. A cool hand gripped his.

He turned to see Rachel.

'Hello, Mister Powers,' she whispered. 'I am so glad you could come to the meeting.'

# CHAPTER 13

'It's Lawless by name and lawless by nature,' said the Professor with relish. 'At this point in time there isn't a tougher town in the whole of the West.'

'It sounds a dandy place,' said Saul drily. 'You reckon this is where I'll find Ben Rockwell?'

'No doubt about it. According to this communication I have received from the Pinkerton's, Rockwell has a big ranch outside the town. He's grown rich and become a cattle baron.'

'Strange when you think how the gang turned out,' said Saul. 'Lew O'Hara became a saloon keeper, Charlie Gideon became a half-crazy bandit on the run, the Cochise Kid carried on bein' the Cochise Kid – an' now Rockwell's become a cattleman. I wonder what happened to Jess Nathan.' 'We'll worry about him after we've crossed Rockwell off the list,' the Professor said. 'From what I hear that's going to be a tall order. According to this letter, Rockwell practically runs the whole territory round Lawless and he uses the town as he pleases. His cowboys "hurrah" it regularly, and no one dare stop them. They've had three marshals in the last twelve months.

There's all sorts of rumours about Rockwell. They say he built up his herd by rustling and he's grown fat on contracts to supply the Indian reservation with beef, only those contracts are crooked and he gets paid double for each beast. It seems nothing can be done because everybody who matters is on his payroll.

'It's going to be a tough job for you, Saul. It

won't be a straight fight like it was with the others. He lives in a ranch that's guarded like an army fort, and when he does come into Lawless he's surrounded by a bodyguard. I think you'd better keep the name of Andrew Druce for a while.'

'So when do we leave for Lawless?' asked Saul.

'Today,' the Professor replied.

'Okay. I just wanna go an' say goodbye to someone.'

'I guess I've got to pull outa Conquest,' he told Rachel when he reached the covered wagon by the mission tent. 'I'm sure sorry to be leavin' so soon, but it's sorta business. I hope when it's over we'll meet up again.'

'Is it ever over?' sighed the girl, looking away from the white-haired young man with the brilliant blue eyes. 'Or will there be more business after that, and then more business?'

Saul looked down at the hat in his hands. ' I guess it would be kinda hard to explain it to you. You see...'

'Please don't bother to tell me,' she said suddenly, turning and giving him a tight smile. 'I don't want to pry into your affairs. After all, we are just a couple of strangers who met on the trail. We have no call over each other. I – I wish you lucky.'

'Rachel,' began Saul. 'There's so much...'

'Why, here's the Padre,' she interrupted brightly. 'Saul is leaving us.'

'I'm sure sorry to hear that,' exclaimed the preacher. 'I was hopin' that come another meetin' I'd have you up there 'fessin' your sins.' He laughed. 'Where are you headin' for, son?'

'A town called Lawless.'

'Godspeed then.' He gripped Saul's hand, then watched him walk down the street to where the distant figure of the Professor was waiting.

'I'm sorry he's leavin' so soon,' the preacher said, turning and looking at his daughter. 'But we may see him again. I've been figurin' that Lawless sure would have a harvest of souls waitin't be saved.'

\* \* \*

Lawless lived up to its name the first night Saul spent there. Tired after the long journey, he went to bed early in his room at the Lawless Palace Hotel. He had just pulled the blankets over him and was checking that the Colt Frontier was within easy reach under his pillow when he heard the unmistakable crash of shotgun.

Jumping out of bed he ran to the window, the .44 in his hand. The street was lit only by the light that streamed from the Wheel of Fortune Saloon opposite. By it Saul saw the figure of a man writhing on the street. The only other sign of life was a number of passers-by hurrying away from the victim of the blast.

Saul hastily pulled on his Levis, then climbed out through his window and ran to the spot where the body lay.

'Where'd it get you?' he said, bending over a man about the same age as himself on whose jacket was pinned a marshal's badge.

'I took it in the legs,' he gasped. 'I feel I'm done for...'

'Never say that until you're in Boothill,' said Saul, trying to see the extent of the wounds. All he could make out was a pool of blood gleaming in the saloon light. 'Just hang on, friend, an' I'll go an' fetch the doc.'

The marshal shook his head.

'If you leave me, they'll finish...' His voice sank to a whisper.

'You there, git!'

Saul looked up. Two men in range riding outfits were looking down at him. One had a scatter gun cradled in his arms.

'Go on, you heard,' said the second. 'Leave that crittur for us an' forget you sawanythin'.'

'I figure he needs a doc pronto,' said Saul, his pulses racing with the sick feeling of excitement he had come to recognise as a gunfighting symptom.

'Vamoose, or you'll need a doc, too,' said the man, raising the ugly gun barrel.

At that moment Saul straightened up. The Colt exploded and the man with the gun gave a high-pitched scream. The other turned and bolted into the shadows.

'I'll worry about him later,' said Saul to the marshal. 'Now I'm goin' to take you to a doc. Can you tell me where there is one?'

'House on the next corner,' muttered the wounded man. 'It's got a sign.'

Saul slipped his arms under the prostrate man and lifted him. As he was moved he gave a stifled cry of agony. Saul began a slow walk down the dark street. It was strangely deserted, but Saul had the uncanny feeling there were eyes watching him from the darkest shadows.

He laid the man down as gently as he could when he reached the corner house. A dim light burned in the interior. He knocked on the door with his gun butt.

'Open up,' he called. 'I got a dyin' man out here.' There was no response, though Saul thought he saw a vague shadow at one of the windows.

'If you don't open up, I'm gonna put a bullet through the lock,' he shouted in desperation. The door opened slightly and a woman's voice said: 'Go away, the doctor's not here.'

'But here's a man needin' help. Let me bring him in.'

The door started to close and Saul thought he heard a whisper from behind it. He jumped forward and pushed it inwards before the lock could click. In the hallway beyond stood the woman and a grey-haired man with gold pince-nez.

'A damn fine doctor you are,' snapped Saul. 'Now get to work on that fella or I'll blow you apart for the cowardly yeller skunk that you are.'

'You don't understand,' retorted the doctor. 'It's dangerous...it's death...'

'I understand all right, an' I guess you're facin' death either way now. I'm not foolin',' and he jabbed the barrel of the Colt hard into the doctor's stomach.

'All right, all right,' he gagged. 'Lift him in, and then for God's sake get him outahere.'

Saul picked up the marshal, who was now unconscious, and took him inside. Gun in hand he watched while the doctor began to staunch the flow of blood from the multiple wounds.

'He'll live,' he said at length, straightening and wiping his hands. 'Now get him outa here before they raze the house.'

'Where does he live?'

'He's got a room back the marshal's office.'

'Okay, you're gonna carry him there.'

'I can't. It would be suicide.'

'Like I said, it will be either way. I've got to be ready in case they try to get him again, so I can't carry him. Come on, now.'

Cursing, the doctor picked up the patient and carried him into the night. Saul followed, his gun ready for instant use until they reached the clapboard building with the word 'Marshal' painted on the side.

Thanks, doc,' he said when the wounded man was laid on the bed. 'What do I owe you?'

'Go to hell,' snapped the doctor.

On the bed the marshal groaned and his eyelids fluttered.

'How are you makin' out, old son?' asked Saul.

'Guess I'll be okay,' came the weak reply. 'Thanks for what you did, stranger.'

Saul put a pannikin of water to his lips.

'Know who did it?'

'It was one of the Star and Bar mob. I'd given 'em a warning...one of 'em got me from behind.'

'Well, that score's settled,' said Saul grimly.

'I should have known it would come to this,' muttered the marshal. 'I was a durned fool to take the job on. I was handy with a gun an' I thought I could handle it.' His white lips curled into an ironical smile. 'There ain't a man born that can handle this town...not with the Star and Bar mob.'

'Is the Star and Bar Rockwell's ranch?'

'Sure is. An' I guess this is his town. Marshals are just appointed to be gunned down.'

'It would seem that way,' Saul agreed. 'Still, I wouldn't mind givin' it a try.'

'You must be crazy.'

'Maybe I am.' Saul bent down and took the star from the wounded man's coat.

\* \* \*

'It seems an odd idea,' said the Professor as he stood in the marshal's office the next morning. 'You're just asking for trouble.'

'That's it, Professor,' said Saul. He was sitting back with his boots resting comfortably on the marshal's battered desk. On his shirt gleamed the five pointed star.

'The mayor's confirmed the appointment. Guess he was only too glad that anyone should take the job. Fifty bucks a month an' half the fines. But it does give me a chance to get at Rockwell. It was one of his boys that shot Jim Butterfield last night. Not that he'll do it again. I hear his body just vanished during the night.'

'So you're marshal of Lawless,' mused the

Professor. 'I must confess it sounds good...'

'It'd look fine in headlines,' said Saul, his expression blank. 'With guns blazing, the marshal of Lawless...I can see it now.'

The Professor ignored the remark.

'All right,' he said. 'Maybe it'll work. But remember you ain't takin' on a man single-handed, you're takin' on a highly organised gang.'

'I ain't liable to forget it,' Saul said.

During the day there were many curious glances through the door of the marshal's office. The word of the night's events had got around, and now it was being whispered that the new marshal was a famous gunfighter. As the morning passed an air of anticipation grew. At nightfall the marshal was supposed to make a round of the town's saloons and sporting houses, and bets were being laid as to how he would make out when faced by the wild element which frequented these establishments.

At noon Saul walked out into the street, then began a slow tour of the town, which in the daylight seemed strangely peaceful.

A few people greeted him with a grin and a 'Howdy, marshal,' but otherwise Saul's stroll was uneventful. As he walked his eyes were busy taking mental note of the narrow alleys and back streets, and the various exits of the buildings which he would have to enter on his patrol.

In his room behind the office the ex-marshal woke from fitful sleep when Saul entered to see if he needed anything.

'I gotta give you a word of advice,' he said hoarsely. 'The two marshals before me were both shot down by a trick...' and for a minute he continued muttering to Saul.

Thanks,' said Saul when he'd finished. Til be watchin' for that.'

At sundown Lawless came to life. Cowpunchers rode in and tethered their horses to the hitching rails in front of the saloons that lined a wide stretch of sun-hardened mud known locally as Good Time Street. In their hotel rooms the professional gamblers rose from their beds and dressed carefully for the night's play. Here and there a honky tonk piano struck up, and soon a band was in full swing at the Queen of Hearts Theatre where numerous young ladies danced on the stage for the edification of the whooping patrons.

At about nine Saul climbed to his feet and eased the gun in his low holster.

'Here goes,' he said to the Professor. 'Better keep your notebook ready. Somethin' tells me it's gonna be an unlucky night.'

# CHAPTER 14

Silence fell on the Wheel of Fortune saloon. An elegant gambler known as the Duke raised his lizard eyes from the faro table and looked at the young figure standing at the door.

'Howdy, marshal,' said the Duke. 'You droppin' in for a game of chance?'

'Not tonight,' said Saul, looking round the quiet assembly. 'Guess I'm takin' my chances elsewhere.'

The Duke smiled thinly.

'I'm sure glad you got a sense of humour,' he said. 'The bets are against you in this town tonight. Maybe it's because you interfered in somethin' that was not your concern last night.'

'I hope you ain't got too much staked,' said Saul. 'I kinda thrive on interferin'.'

'He's got guts,' said the Duke as he returned to the game. 'A pity...'

Everywhere Saul's entrance had the same effect, a sudden death of conversation and curious, speculative looks.

The first trouble came when Saul entered the Maverick Bar at the end of Good Time Street. As he walked in, a drunk turned from the bar with a revolver in his hand and a murderous gleam in his bloodshot eye.

'Dance, you son of a bitch,' he yelled. The gun blasted and a slug splintered the floor a couple of feet from Saul's foot.

'Dance, damn you,' he yelled and fired again.

This time the bullet hole was closer.

The customers had quietly backed out of the line of fire and were now watching the drama with silent enjoyment. Through his narrowed eyes Saul saw the bartender could easily put the drunk out of action with a well aimed blow across the bar. Instead he preferred to await the outcome.

'Marshal, I told you to dance.' The drunk pulled the trigger once more, and this time the bullet hit the floor between Saul's feet. 'Nice gun work considerin' he's got a skinful,' murmured a customer.

Still the new marshal of Lawless stood as though petrified.

'Goddam it, I'll make you dance – or die,' shouted the drunk, tears of frustration welling in his eyes. The barrel of his gun rose ominously.

'I'll tell you somethin',' said Saul quietly.

'What?' demanded the drunk.

'I ain't no shakes at dancin' – but I'll show you what I am good at.'

His hand gripped the bone handle of his gun and in a movement too fast for the onlookers to follow, raised it to eye level and fired. The slug caught the drunk's pistol and sent it spinning out of his hand. With a wail of dismay he raised his bloodied fingers to his mouth. Then his eyes widened with fear as Saul slowly bolstered the smoking Frontier and began walking across the floor.

'I didn't mean no harm, marshal, honest I didn't,' the drunk stammered. 'It was just my joke...just my joke...' He cringed back as Saul reached the bar, but the expected blow never came. Instead Saul's fist pistoned out and caught the bartender full in the mouth.

He staggered back under the shock, crashing against the shelf of bottles which fell to the floor in a crescendo of breaking glass.

'You could have stopped that fella firin' at me

any time you liked,' said Saul. 'Next time control your customers.'

As Saul stepped into the cool night air a buzz rose in the bar behind him – a buzz of admiration for his skill with his gun coupled with laughter at the plight of the bartender who was tenderly feeling a wide gap in his front teeth.

'I see you have won Round One,' remarked the Professor when Saul returned to the marshal's office. 'When does Round Two take place?'

' 'Bout midnight,' Saul replied.

'I trust you won't get carried away by the idea of being the guardian of law and order in this town. Remember, it's Rockwell you came for.'

'Don't fret,' said Saul, sinking behind the desk. 'Not a day, not an hour passes when I don't remember. All my life I've thought of nothin' else but revenge. In fact, I guess I won't know what to do when it's over.'

'That'll take care of itself,' said the Professor. 'You'll be the top gun in the country. The West will be at your feet. There'll be as much money as you want...'

'You mean by doin' a stage tour of the East like Hickok?'

'Why not? You'll be a celebrity so we may as well cash in on it.'

Behind the blue-tinted glasses the Professor's eyes gleamed. 'I've always dreamed of building up the top gun of them all...'

'I thought all this was for my father's memory,' Saul said.

'That's just it,' said the Professor hastily. 'If your father could have lived he would have been a legend now. You have carried on his skill for him, and I am proud that in some small way I have been able to help you do so. I shall be repaid when the last of his killers meets his end, why else should I have spent this time and money?'

'Why indeed,' said Saul. 'I guess it's just that I don't figure you, Professor.'

'Don't worry about that, Saul. You just stick to the shooting and I'll do the figuring.'

\* \* \*

At midnight Saul got from behind his desk, stretched himself and began his second patrol of the town. From the sounds he heard he knew that the town had livened up. From Good Time Street came hot gusts of music, the yells of celebrating cowboys and the occasional sound of breaking glass. As Saul prowled past a saloon in the shadows the batwing doors suddenly parted and a limp figure flew through the air to land on all fours at the new marshal's feet.

'An' next time pay for your liquor!' yelled the bouncer.

The bum looked up. 'Goo' night, marshal,' he slurred and promptly went to sleep. Saul walked on grinning. As he reached a small saloon on the corner of Good Time Street and a narrow alley, he heard a scream and then a couple of shots. He turned to dive through the doors of the saloon, then checked himself remembering the advice Jim Butterfield had given him that morning. Instead of running up the steps to the doors of the saloon, Saul sprinted round the side of it and down the alley. Thankful he had had the foresight to reconnoitre earlier on, he found the back entrance to the saloon.

He cat-footed across a small storeroom and then opened a door that led into the long bar. A strange tableaux met his gaze. Three men crouched in a semi-circle before the swinging doors leading on to Good Time Street. Each had a pistol raised, ready to blast the next person to enter.

'Drop your hardware,' snapped Saul, 'an' raise your hands. Make any other move an' I'll shoot to kill.'

One after the other the guns hit the floor.

'Right, turn round and line up against the wall,' commanded Saul. Slowly the men turned, dismay and anger written on their faces. Saul looked them over to make sure they were not carrying any other weapon.

'Keep your hands elevated,' he went on. 'Just cause a trick like that worked a couple of times in the past don't mean to say the third time'll be lucky. I guess you thought I'd run in like the other marshals when I heard them decoy shots. I also reckon I can take it that you critturs are from the Star and Bar.'

They looked at him sullenly.

'So what do you aim to do, marshal?' demanded one.

'Take you in.'

'What for? We ain't broke no law.'

'Let's see – I reckon disturbance of the peace will just about fit the bill,' said Saul. 'Now, get goin'. Walk three abreast in the direction of the jail. Try dodgin' an' I'll blow the heads off your shoulders – an' there's nothin' I'd rather do than that just now. So if you wanta please me, try makin' a break.'

In silence the small group crunched along Good Time Street and on to the small brick jailhouse which stood next to the marshal's office.

When the cell door clanged shut on the three prisoners, the one who had spoken before said: 'They was takin' bets on how long you'd last, marshal. I said a couple days an' I reckon my money's still safe. One thing about Ben Rockwell, he never lets his boys down. He'll come an' get us out, an' I sure hate to be in your boots when he does.'

\* \* \*

The news of the arrest of the three would-be assassins spread like a prairie blaze through Lawless and the young marshal was looked at with a new respect, and at the same time a certain sympathy. Many old-timers declared that to take in three of the Star and Bar boys was the same as asking for a one-way ticket for Boothill.

Saul, if he knew of these prophecies of gloom, certainly did not let them reflect in his face the next morning when he opened up the marshal's office.

'Professor,' he said when the tall, flabby writer called on him after breakfast, 'I feel kinda good today. I reckon this job sorta suits me. I reckon I'd like to spend some of my pay on some new clothes. The mayor gave me an advance, an' I reckon I ain't dressed respectable enough for the office I hold.' He looked down at his faded Levis.

'I think that is an excellent idea,' said the Professor lighting one of his slim cigars. 'All the great gunfighters were fancy dressers and you should be in the tradition. With the reputation you have now you owe – you should look the part.'

'Right then, let's step along to the store an' get fitted out.'

An hour later Saul returned to the office in a fine black suit, a dark blue satin waistcoat and a shirt of dazzling white silk. At his neck there was a black ribbon tie and on his feet were shoes of the finest gleaming leather. The only things that remained from his old worn outfit were the heavy gun belt, the Colt slung far down on his thigh, and the nickel star of office on the lapel of his coat.

'When we find ourselves in a place that has a photographer, we must have your likeness taken,' said the Professor. 'To Eastern eyes you look like the quintessence of the successful gun-fighter.'

Saul smiled slightly. 'It wasn't the reason I got these clothes,' he said. 'I – aw, let's skip it.'

'What are you going to do with those Star and

Bar men?'

'I'm gonna take 'em before the judge an' get 'em fined twenty bucks a head for disturbing the peace. That's if he's got the guts to fine them. But I reckon things might develop some before then.'

'That could be,' the Professor agreed. 'The word going round town is that Rockwell will ride in and get them out. In fact if he doesn't he'll lose face. It could be your chance to confront him, but be careful, he'll have his bodyguard with him.'

'I'll be ready,' said Saul.

A couple of hours later a red-haired man in range-riding clothes burst into the office.

'Marshal, my name's Glen,' he said. 'I got a small place to the north. As I was comin' in to town I saw Rockwell an' his band headin' this way. I guess you know why they're comin'. I managed to get ahead of them. I've come to warn you because I plumb admire the way you've gone about bein' marshal an' lockin' up them three coyotes.'

'It's mighty good of you to warn me,' said Saul. 'I need a few friends in this town.'

'Well, count on me. Anythin' I could do to help get rid of that goddam Rockwell an' his murderin' nightriders I'd do. This could be a good town an' a good territory if it weren't for them. They rule by fear, marshal. No one dare do anythin'.'

'Yeah, I saw that the first night I was here,' said Saul, remembering the terror of the doctor at having to tend one of the Star and Bar victims. 'But do you mean that about doin' anythin' to help?'

'Gosh darn it, I sure do. I may be crazy, but I can't take it no more. They've been rustlin' my beeves sure as there's fire in hell.'

'All right, Glen,' said Saul. 'You're a temporary deputy marshal of Lawless from now on. All I want you to do is sit on the jail roof when the mob rides in, an' if anyone draws a bead on me when I'm not lookin' shoot 'em down.'

'It's a deal,' cried the rancher. 'Martha would go screamin' loco if she knew, but I reckon there comes a time when a man's gotta make a stand.'

Saul leaned forward and clasped his hand.

'Could I have your full name, please,' asked the Professor from his seat in the corner.

Glen looked at him puzzled.

'He's all right,' said Saul. 'He writes for the papers.'

'It's Maddox Glen,' said the rancher. 'My ranch is the Lazy-Y.' The Professor wrote in his notebook.

'You'd better get up on that roof,' said Saul. 'It's flat, so try an' keep outa sight behind the parapet.'

To their ears came the sound of distant hooves and a wild yelling.

'Here they come,' said Saul. A strange, cold look had come into his intense blue eyes. 'I'm sorta lookin' forward to meetin' Ben Rockwell.'

\* \* \*

Yelling at the tops of their voices and shooting pistols off above their heads, the band of Star and Bar riders swept down the main street of Lawless to halt in a swirling cloud of dust in front of the small brick jail. In the middle of the band, on a large black gelding, was Ben Rockwell. He was a slim upright man with a military bearing and a hairline moustache across his upper lip.

On the steps of the jail stood another slim man in stylish black trousers, a dark satin waistcoat and silk shirt. Saul had prudently taken his coat off to allow his gun hand maximum freedom.

For a moment there was silence. From the verandahs of Lawless the locals watched with one eye on the riders and one eye on the nearest piece of cover. Ben Rockwell urged his horse forward until he was facing Saul.

'I've come for my boys,' he said in a flat voice.

Behind the barred windows the three prisoners grinned at their comrades.

'You can take 'em,' said Saul, 'if you pay me sixty dollars.'

There was another silence, then Rockwell said in a voice that one might use explaining something to a backward child.

'Do you know who I am, marshal?'

'Reckon you're Ben Rockwell,' said Saul. 'Reckon you own me sixty dollars in fines for your boys.'

'Get... them... out... of... that... jail... before... I... cut... you down,' hissed the Star and Bar boss in an icy fury.

'I figure you've had a lot of fellas cut down in your time,' said Saul, his piercing gaze on Rockwell's face. 'But you do it at night, an' in the back, an' to guys who can't fight back. At the moment it's daylight, an' I'm town marshal an' it would be murder an' you wouldn't get away with it, even if the military had to come in.'

'Don't gamble on that,' said Rockwell. 'I've got all the witnesses I need whatever happens. Now, for the last time, let my boys out.'

'The fines come to sixty bucks,' said Saul. 'If you want 'em you pay for 'em.'

Rockwell gave an imperceptible sign to one of his men. At that moment a Remington cracked from the roof of the jail. Several mounts reared and one of the riders gave a screech of agony. The gun which he had aiming at Saul dropped to the dust beneath his horse's hooves.

At the sound of the gunshot Saul snatched his Frontier and went into the gunfighter's crouch. The muzzle of the .44 pointed directly at Ben Rockwell, while Saul's eyes remained equally steady on his face.

'If anyone tries that again, your boss is a dead man,' he cried. 'If you think you can help him by drawin' on me save yourselves the effort. If I'm hit the deputy has orders to shoot Rockwell down.'

The ranch boss looked wildly from side to side.

'Goddam you,' he snarled. 'Do you think you'll get away with this?'

'That ain't the question,' said Saul. 'Question is, are you gonna ante up.'

'I'll see you in hell first.'

'I'm gonna give you up to ten,' said Saul, 'to pay up or get back to your ranch. *One...*'

'Now look here...'

'*... two... three...four...*'

A sound of creaking wheels came down the street, but everyone was too intent on the drama to turn.

'*... five... six... seven...*'

'Marshal, I tell you...' began Rockwell, a fine sweat breaking out on his tanned face.

'*... eight... nine...*'

At that moment an old covered wagon with the word 'REPENT' emblazoned on its canvas rolled into view, and a girl's voice cried 'Stop! Stop!'

# CHAPTER 15

Saul ignored the interruption. 'Ten!' he said.

The gun in his hand spat orange flame and Rockwell's Stetson jerked off his head as though plucked by an invisible hand.

'All right,' he cried. 'Take your money.' Putting his hand inside his pocket he pulled out a handful of notes and threw them down. They fluttered to Saul's feet.

'I guess I'd be pretty foolish to bend down to pick them up,' said Saul. 'Get down and give 'em to me proper, Rockwell.'

The Star and Bar boss sat astride his mount as though stunned. Never in his long violent life had he known such humiliation. How he wished the gun at his side was in his hand, but having seen Saul's draw he knew that he would not stand a chance against the white-haired young slinger.

'This game to you,' he said, slowly dismounting. 'But it ain't the last game.'

He did not bend to pick up the scattered notes. He took more money from his pocket and counted out sixty dollars.

'Want a receipt?' asked Saul, taking the wad of money in his left hand. 'Let those guys out, Professor,' he called.

As the men were being released Ben Rockwell smiled faintly, and, speaking in a low voice that did not carry, he said: 'You are a cool one, son. You've bettered me an' I admit it. Tell you what, I have a great use for men like you. Why not join my outfit? You'll earn many times over with me what you get as a marshal in this lousy town. It's a good life on the Star and Bar. What do you say?'

'Nothin' doin'.'

'But why? This ain't no job for a gunhand like you.'

'Because there was once a fella by the name of Luke Powers. That's why.'

Rockwell looked closely into Saul's face.

'You mean...'

Saul nodded slowly.

'Now take your gang back to the Star and Bar,' said Saul. 'They're sorta messin' up the street.'

Without a word Rockwell swung back into the saddle. His men followed at a quick trot. No one spoke until they were out of sight, though all eyes were focussed on the dollars blowing lazily down the street. Then suddenly someone cried, 'Hurrah for the new marshal,' and several voices echoed it in a ragged cheer.

Saul walked over to the mission wagon.

'Hello,' he grinned up at Rachel.

'Hello, Saul,' she said, her hair blowing half across her face in a way that Saul remembered so acutely. 'I'm sorry I cried out. I thought...it doesn't matter. Does that star mean that you've hired your gun to law and order?'

'Don't let us talk about guns,' he begged, swinging up beside her.

'You're right,' said the Padre. 'As marshal you should be able to show us the best place to pitch the tent. I've planned on comin' to this town for sometime. I think it is overdue for some preachin'.'

'If there's a place in the West that needs the Good Word, this is it,' said Saul happily.

From the steps of the jail the Professor looked at

the wagon through his blue spectacles and frowned. In front of him a number of citizens of Lawless were scrabbling after the money fluttering in the wind.

* * *

The next few nights were strangely peaceful for Lawless. No Star and Bar men came into town and the main topic of interest was the Gospel tent where lively meetings were held nightly. Sometimes in their enthusiasm for the Padre's message some citizens discharged their firearms through the canvas roof, but the presence of the slim, black-clad marshal had the effect of curbing these demonstrations.

To a lot of citizens this period of calm was a lull before a storm. Sooner or later Ben Rockwell would strike back at the young man who had publicly humiliated him. The only point worth discussing was when.

On the night after Saul had collected the sixty dollars in such a spectacular way, a group of men met late in his office.

Maddox Glen introduced them in turn, and then said to Saul: 'These fellas are small ranchers like me. For years now we've had to put up with the Star and Bar playin' hell with us. There was no way we could hit back when our beeves were rustled, or when we was cheated over water rights, or when we were forced by blackmail to sell off cheap. If we didn't like it the alternative was to quit our land. Sure, 'way back a few guys protested, but they all got lead poisonin'. We learned the best way was to stay dumb.

'But after what happened outside the jail...well, we reckon we gotta chance after all. If you could give us the lead I figure we'd be happy to be your deputies.'

'What do you have in mind?' Saul asked.

'We know a lot of the cattle Rockwell supplies to the Indian reservation are rustled from the ranches in this territory. If we could get enough evidence we could take it to the State Governor. That's one place where even Rockwell's bribes couldn't save him.'

'That's right,' chimed in another rancher. 'If we could catch Star and Bar men with a herd of stolen cattle we'd have him.'

'How'd you go about that?' asked Saul.

'Well,' said Maddox Glen, 'I reckon how's about the time. I happen to know he's gettin' a big herd together to take to the reservation. His boys ain't comin' into town at the moment, which means they must be on some night work. If we could catch 'em in the act of rustlin'...'

'Sounds all right to me,' said Saul. 'Are your men all agreed?' The dozen men nodded. 'Then I'll swear you in as legal deputies. After that we'd better figure out the best way of goin' about this.'

Two nights later Saul was standing by the entrance of the tent prior to a meeting, when Maddox Glen sidled up to him.

'I've got the word,' he whispered. 'They're movin' a small herd of beeves along my north valley. I reckon if we ride hard we can reach them while they're still on my ranch.'

Without a word Saul turned and followed him. Soon they were galloping along the moonlit trail to the Lazy-Y ranch house. Here the rest of Saul's secret deputies were assembling.

'Now this valley cuts through a plateau like a small canyon,' Glen explained. 'At one end there's a creek, an' on the other side is Star and Bar country. I figure we should be waiting for them at the creek.'

'Some of us should,' said Saul. 'But I want several of you for another job,' and he went on to outline his plan.

\* \* \*

At midnight Saul and six of his men, including Maddox Glen, took up position on the shore of the creek. Before them the valley mouth lay in mysterious shadow.

'All we gotta do now is wait,' said Saul. 'I reckon it won't be too long if my ears hear aright.'

They listened. Faintly on the night wind came the lowing of longhorns and the occasional whicker of a horse.

'They got them beeves on the move all right,' muttered Glen.

The sounds of the unseen herd came closer. Suddenly from the top of the valley walls came the crash of rifle fire. The echo of the shot reverberated in the valley like thunder. Immediately followed the bellowing of terrified Lazy-Y cattle and the curses of the men who had been driving them.

'Good,' said Glen, 'that's got the stampede movin'. Those goddam rustlers won't know what's hit 'em.'

Above the crash of rifles continued. Suddenly from the opening of the valley the watchers saw a dark mass moving swiftly towards the creek. As it came out into the moonlight they could see the forms of cattle racing towards them in terror. Above the sea of tossing heads they could pick out the men on horseback being swept along with the long-horned current.

Just as the leaders of the stampede splashed into the creek, churning the surface to living silver, Saul and his companions fired a volley above their heads. The panic-stricken beasts paused and then tried to retreat, but others behind them pressed on and soon there was a vortex of maddened animals surging in wild confusion at the entrance to the gorge.

The rustlers were trapped on their horses. Unable to escape because of the steep sides of the valley, they were caught like driftwood sucked into a whirlpool.

As Saul and his deputies blazed away in the air they saw a horse and rider suddenly disappear under the waves of cattle. A hideous scream rose above the bellowing, and was abruptly cut off. Now, as prearranged, the men at the cliff tops ceased firing while the men across the creek continued until their guns ran hot. The effect of this was to cause the stampede to surge back into the valley, still with the riders wedged in it.

Saul and his men swung into their saddles and splashed across the creek, driving the herd back up the valley. The Star and Bar men were too busy trying to remain astride their terrified horses to think of firing at the ranchers who were now riding the herd on them. As the frantic rush continued up the valley several more riders were lost beneath the mass of tightly packed steers.

\* \* \*

In the cold light of dawn a group of horsemen rode swiftly along the Lawless trail. Behind each deputy was a lead horse on which sat a Star and Bar man, his hands tied behind his back. Of the original band of twenty who had started out to rustle the Lazy-Y cattle, only twelve remained. The others had perished under the thudding hooves of the panicked steers. By the time the herd had finally ceased its aimless flight the rustlers had lost any inclination to make a stand, especially as they found they were well covered by the rifles of the Lawless deputies.

'Reckon the jail will be jest about burstin'' when we get this lot inside,' said one of the weary riders.

'Reckon we could save space by stringin'' 'em up right now,' said another.

'You can forget that,' said Saul. These coyotes are gonna stand trial fair an' square. We want everythin' to come to light, the rustling, the crooked contracts, the murders. It'll be the end of Rockwell's power here.'

'I hope you're right,' said Maddox Glen. 'But he's a tricky customer an' somethin' in my bones tells me the fight ain't over yet.'

In Lawless the cattle thieves were thrown into the cells of the jail and several deputies were posted as guards. Saul walked slowly into the marshal's office where he had made his quarters. He sat down behind the scarred desk and took a cardboard box of .44-40 centre fire cartridges out of the drawer to refill the empty loops of his gunbelt. Before he could begin his shoulders slumped with fatigue and his head fell on his hands. He did not wake even when there was a drumming of hooves down the main street at dawn.

It was fully daylight when Saul opened his eyes. He rose and stretched himself, then went and put a battered coffee-pot on the stove in the corner, bending down to coax some flame out of the grey ashes.

The door of the office opened. He spun round, and his face relaxed into a smile when he saw the visitor.

'Hello, Padre, this is an early call,' he said. Then he noticed the strained look on the preacher's face. 'Is there something wrong?'

'There is something dreadfully wrong,' he replied. 'Rachel has been kidnapped.'

'What...'

'A short while ago two men came to the wagon. They had guns. They gagged me and tied me up with rope – I've only just managed to get free – and they took Rachel at pistol point. I heard them make her get on a horse, and then they galloped off.'

'It was Rockwell?'

The preacher nodded his head.

'He took her as a hostage,' he said.

# CHAPTER 16

'You've got to get her back, Saul,' said the Padre.

The young marshal nodded. 'You got an idea where they took her?'

'I'd say by the sound of the hoofbeats they went up the street to the north.'

'All right,' he said. 'I'm on my way. I guess you better wait for her here—an' pray.'

'You know, Saul, she...' but whatever he was going to say was lost in the slam of the office door. Outside Saul went to the jail and quickly explained what had happened to Maddox Glen.

'Riders did go past a while back,' he said.' If they're ridin' north I guess they could be headin' to the Star and Bar ranch. Maybe Rockwell reckons he'll be able to hold on there. Maybe he figures he can do some sorta deal with you with Miss Rachel as a hostage. He musta found out she was sweet on you. Or maybe...' He did not continue.

'Maybe it'll be a straight act of revenge,' Saul muttered. 'He might kill her to even the score with me.'

'Don't think of that,' said Glen. 'Let's get after her.'

A minute later the two men were galloping along the trail that led north from Lawless in the direction of the Star and Bar.

Saul knew that his only chance was to overtake the kidnappers before they reached the shelter of the ranch. Rockwell would still have enough of his gang left to defend it against them, and he dreaded the idea of Rachel being at the centre of a battle. Mercilessly he plied the quirt which dangled from his wrist to the lathered flanks of his mount.

Beside him Maddox Glen's spurs had left bloody weals on his horse's hide.

Soon the trail began to go uphill and the breathing of the two horses became agonised.

'By the look of the dust there's been hosses passin' this way pretty recent,' shouted Glen as they breasted the rise. Ahead the trail ran straight across the flat top of a small plateau, 'If they've come this way we'll maybe see them when we reach the other side of this tableland.'

Saul's quirt fell again and his horse thundered forward, its nostrils dilated, its eyes wild and its mane streaming in the wind. Behind came Glen, leaning forward in the stirrups like a jockey.

As he rode at breakneck speed Saul's eyes were glued to the trail but in his mind there was a picture of Rachel as he best remembered her, a strand of her hair blowing across her face and that look of warmth in her violet eyes which he had never seen before in any woman. At the thought of her in the hands of a murderer like Rockwell his nerves tensed so that he felt physical pain in his chest and stomach. It was a spasm of fear which was new to him, far worse than the sensation he had felt when he slowly walked up Silver Street to Lew O'Hara.

They reached the opposite edge of the plateau and here they reined up. Below they saw a grassy plain undulating to the horizon through which the trail curved like a fine white thread. About a couple of miles along it there was a moving cloud of pale dust.

'There they are,' Saul cried. 'If we go like hell we can catch them up.'

'An' give 'em good warning we're comin',' said

Maddox Glen. 'Now look, the trail curves because in the winter part of the plain floods. If we go straight we might be able to head them off. See that dried-up watercourse. It's a torrent in winter. That leads to the creek. If we follow it there's a chance we just might reach the old ferry ahead of them. Once they're across that they're on Star and Bar land...'

Before he finished Saul urged his mount forward and down the track that twisted down the steep slope. It was a miracle the animal kept its balance. Several times it slid on the corners of the zig-zag path, sending miniature avalanches of stones down the plateau side.

Encouraging it with curses and endearments, Saul rode with a skill which he never realised he possessed. In desperation he whipped the poor beast down narrow ridges which normally he would have approached at a slow walk. The last stage of the descent was made with the horse sliding on its haunches.

As it righted itself Maddox Glen flashed past, waving to Saul to follow him. Turning off the trail the two riders hurtled across open country. At any moment one of the mounts could put its hoof in a prairie dog burrow and bring down its rider. But Saul knew this was no time for caution. Only one thing mattered and that was speed.

Soon they were racing along the dry watercourse. Not only did this take them more directly to the creek than the trail, but its chaparral-covered banks sheltered them from view.

To Saul's dismay he sensed his horse was beginning to fail. It still galloped gamely but its legs were slowing and the heaving of the fine chest as it fought for air was becoming irregular.

'Not much farther now,' shouted Glen.

Saul's horse almost stumbled, then picked up its flying gait again.

'Come on, my beauty,' Saul hissed in its ear.

'Just keep a-goin' an' I'll buy you the best corn in Lawless. Keep a-going, goddam you.'

The course began to curve gently and ahead they glimpsed the sparkle of early sunlight on water. They had reached the creek.

'The ferry's upstream a mite on the left,' Glen said.

At that moment Saul felt his mount fall away from him. The poor beast crashed into the soft sand of the watercourse, sending Saul sprawling over its head. Glen reined up as he struggled to his feet.

'Okay?'

'Yeah. The crittur's plumb ridden out though.' For a moment he tugged at the reins but the foam flecked animal rolled its eyes and refused to budge. Glen swung down from his horse which was almost in the same state as Saul's.

'Come on on foot,' said Glen. 'It'll give us a better chance of surprisin' them.'

'Careful with the gunplay,' panted Saul as they sprinted to the glitter of the creek. 'I don't want Rachel harmed none.'

The rancher nodded, saving his breath. Next moment they left the course and found themselves on the muddy margin of the creek. About a hundred yards along it Saul saw the ferry. It was a flat platform mounted on a raft of logs. Ropes stretched across the creek and it was by these the ferry passengers had to haul their crude craft across the wide stretch of water.

As Saul looked he saw three horses and riders draw up in a swirl of dust. His heart beat faster when he saw one of the riders was Rachel. Her hands were knotted behind her back with her scarf. Her horse must have been led, which would explain how Saul and his deputy had managed to catch up with the party.

Rockwell and his henchmen dismounted. The

latter began to lead the horses on to the ferry.

'Now,' hissed Saul.

Crouching almost double, and with the Colt Frontier in his hand, he raced along the shore of the creek. Behind ran Maddox Glen holding a Sharps-Borchardt at waist level.

Saul was still about fifty yards away when the Star and Bar rider, who was now on the raft trying to pacify one of the horses, looked up and saw them.

'Look out,' he yelled to Rockwell who held the cheek strap of Rachel's horse. Rockwell spun round and, seeing Saul, dived for his gun. At the same time his companion took aim.

Before he could pull the trigger Maddox Glen fired his Sharps from the hip. He never knew what damage the heavy bullet caused. At the sound of the shot the restless horse reared, its front hooves pawing the air furiously. Then, as it descended, its left shoe thudded sickeningly into its master's skull, toppling him backwards into the creek.

Meanwhile Rockwell had raised his gun and fired a couple of shots in rapid succession at Saul. The range was still too far for accuracy with a revolver and both slugs passed him harmlessly.

Knowing he would have to get closer if he was to fire without endangering Rachel, Saul continued sprinting forward. When Rockwell saw the fate of his companion, he swung his pistol round and pointed it up at the girl.

'Stop where you are or I'll blast her,' he yelled.

Saul came to a helpless stop, lowering his gun to his side.

'That's better,' Rockwell shouted. 'I guess I still hold the aces.'

'I've sworn to kill you, but if you let her go free you can take a hoss across on the ferry an' I swear not to follow you,' said Saul.

Ben Rockwell laughed.

'You ain't exactly in the position to make bargains,' he said. Throw down your guns.' Carefully Saul tossed his gun on the soft ground a couple of yards in front of him. Behind he heard a faint thud as Glen's heavy rifle fell.

Rockwell swung the gun from Rachel and covered Saul and his companion. A grim smile lit his thin face.

'Say goodbye to the world, boys,' he said. 'First you, Glen; then you, Powers.'

With deliberate slowness he stretched his arm out to full length and aimed. 'If you keep still I'll let you have it nice an' quick, through the head,' he hissed.

Frozen in his tracks, Saul looked past the sadistic boss of the Star and Bar and saw Rachel dig the sharp heels of her riding boots into the sides of her horse.

At the unexpected pain the animal skittered, knocking against Rockwell's back and upsetting his balance. As he rocked the gun exploded and the bullet whined past Saul like an infuriated hornet.

At that moment Saul threw himself forward. His outstretched hand closed on the butt of the Colt where he had so carefully thrown it. From his prone position he fired as Rockwell regained his balance.

The inbred instinct of the gunfighter did not desert Saul even for such a fast and difficult shot. Slowly, slowly Rockwell began to collapse. His knees bent and his body twisted with a strange grace as though he was underwater. As he sagged he continued to jerk the trigger of his pistol. The bullets went wild, but to his horror Saul saw he was trying to bring the gun into line with Rachel. Then came a click as the hammer fell on a spent cartridge. Rockwell mouthed a curse, and sprawled lifeless.

Saul turned to see if Glen had been hurt by Rockwell's shot, but the rancher was calmly picking up his rifle.

'Guess... that's... the... job... finished, marshal,' he said with a grin.

'Reckon it is, deputy,' Saul replied as his fingers began to untie the knots in Rachel's scarf.

\* \* \*

It was several days after the demise of Ben Rockwell. Saul approached the Padre's old Conestoga wagon and his blue eyes reflected his pleasure when he saw Rachel appear.

'Hello, hero,' she smiled. For a moment she looked at him, a quizzical expression on her mobile features. 'There's something missing,' she said. 'You look different. Why, you've forgotten to pin on your star.'

Saul shook his head. 'I took it off,' he said. 'I reckon now Jim Butterfield can hobble around a bit I best give it back to him.'

'So you're no longer marshal of Lawless,' said Rachel. 'What now, young man? More business?'

He nodded.

'More gun business?'

'Maybe.'

'So the Professor has found your next victim. Who are you going to shoot next?'

'Don't say it like that,' Saul protested. 'I've tried to explain, but it's somethin' you can't understand...! don't reckon anyone understands 'cept the Professor.'

'Oh, you fool, you deluded fool,' cried Rachel. 'Don't you know what's happening to you? Don't you realise you are destroying yourself, that every time you use your gun you are burying yourself further in guilt.'

'I know how you feel about it, 'specially with your Pa bein' a preacher an' all. You could only see it my way if you'd seen your father gunned down when you was a kid. Whatever you say, I can't forget that.'

'Of course you can't, Saul, but don't you realise that you have been exploited because of it. First your mother brought you up to think of nothing but revenge. You didn't stand a chance against her and her load of hatred. She didn't bring you up as if you were a natural kid, but as her instrument of retribution. And then your Professor came along and took over.'

'He was the only guy that ever helped me any,' said Saul. 'He provided me my gun, an' money...'

'And look what you provided him. Just the chance he was looking for. I've checked up on Jonathan Coffin. He's grown rich writing about you. I showed you an article once in the *Frontier Journal*. That's just one of a hundred. Why, there's even a book about you back East.

'Don't you understand there is a great deal of money to be earned writing about the West. And more than money, fame! Look how Ned Buntline made a reputation for himself by writing about Wyatt Earp, the Colonel George Ward Nicholas for his reports on Wild Bill Hickok. But the difference between them is this – they wrote about events as they happened and about men who were already gunfighters. Jonathan Coffin makes events happen. He has moulded you to be the ideal hero for his dispatches. One day he'll take you on tour of the East so people can gape at a real live gunslinger. Do you really believe he did it because he knew your father?'

'I've wondered about that,' Saul admitted. 'He certainly didn't remember my Pa was a left-handed shot. He shoulda known that.'

'I'll bet he never set eyes on him,' Rachel declared. 'It was just his explanation to you. What he wanted was a fast kid he could build into a second Hickok. And you weren't the first by any means. There was Frankie Kelso, and then Grant Hicks. Whatever happened to Grant Hicks?'

'He was shot in a bar in Nogales,' Saul replied

automatically.

'So you are his third protégé, and his best. I'd say the other two did it because they wanted fame. You were much better material, all your life you've been taught to think of revenge until you were nothing but a hand of vengeance...'

Saul started at the phrase. 'Those are the same words the Professor used once,' he mused.

'Can't you see it yourself?' Rachel continued. 'Do you know what it's like to laugh like other people? Do you ever sing as you ride along? Have you ever got pleasure from anything but that damned gun at your side? Do you know what it's like to be alive?'

Saul struggled for words to reply.

'I know it must seem that way to you, but – but it's somethin' that's inside me; an' you explainin' what you think it is don't make it any different,' he said. 'I've got to go after Jesse Nathan, that's all I know. I don't give a goddam what the Professor writes. I can't help it if you think I am some sort of tool. All that matters is that I even up the score for my Dad. Words can't alter that feelin'.'

'So you are going to go after this man whoever he is?'

Saul nodded.

'No matter what I say – no matter how important it is for me that you get off what Jonathan Coffin calls your vengeance trail?'

'I'm sorry,' muttered Saul with a sigh. 'But that's the way it is.'

There was a silence.

'Guess I'll be on my way,' he said, turning.

'Saul Powers,' said Rachel solemnly. 'I warn you, I am a very determined woman and I shall do everything a mortal can to stop you. Don't you realise...?'

'Yes,' said Saul. 'But I can't be anythin' but what I am, no matter how I might wish things were different. Goodbye, Rachel.'

She smiled slightly but said nothing.

As he walked away his hand brushed against the smooth bone handle of the Colt Frontier as though seeking reassurance.

# CHAPTER 17

Leading his heavily packed burro, Yellow Dog, the Indian guide, paced tirelessly across the desert floor. Behind him rode Saul and the Professor.

'How much more to go?' demanded the latter.

'Little way now,' grunted Yellow Dog. 'Someone follow us on horse.'

Saul strained his ears but heard nothing except the sound of their own mounts in the hot solitude of the Painted Desert. It was here, in the wilderness of incredible natural colour and grotesque rock formation, that Saul expected to find Jesse Nathan, the last of the five men responsible for his father's brutal death.

Once again it had been the Professor who had discovered his whereabouts. It seemed that Nathan had become a prospector and for the last few years had been hoping to strike it rich in the Painted Desert.

Leaving Lawless, and travelling to San Juan, the last outpost on the edge of the desert, the two men found Yellow Dog. This elderly Indian made a meagre living by taking supplies out to the few prospectors who spent their days in the mirage-haunted wilderness. He had agreed to lead the strangers to Jesse Nathan for a couple of dollars.

'What is Señor Nathan like?' Saul asked the Indian.

'Señor Nathan is loco,' said the Indian. 'But him no fool.'

'If he's no fool, how can he be loco?'

'Any man live in desert, him loco. Work all day

in sun, come town twice a year...for what? Maybe one day him find gold, maybe one day him die. But Nathan still think fast. No man cheat him. Just loco about gold.'

He shrugged his shoulders to show his contempt for the obsession of the palefaces.

Now to Saul's ears came the faint sound of a distant horse. He turned in the saddle and looked back along the trail. Coming round a tall, wind-eroded column of ochre-hued rock he saw a horse and rider.

'Well, I'll be goddamed,' he muttered as he screwed his eyes up against the glare.

The Professor paused in the lighting of one of his slender cigars and turned his blue-spectacled gaze on the lone traveller.

'That bitch!' he spat.

Saul turned his mount and rode back to meet Rachel who was approaching at a fast trot. She wore a long riding-habit and a white sombrero.

'Hello, Saul,' she said quietly, reining up.

'Rachel, what are you doing here?'

'I warned you I would try and stop you from killing this man. I have come to warn him...'

'But how did you know how to find us?'

'It was easy. I learned that you had taken the stage from Lawless to San Juan, so I followed on the next one. In San Juan I found it common talk that you had left with an Indian to find Nathan. So I hired a horse and followed the trail I was told you had taken.'

'But it was damned dangerous for you.'

She smiled. 'I may be an evangelist's daughter, but I can take care of myself. I've been in this type of country many times when the Padre visited isolated mining settlements. And I can shoot quite well.' She touched a Remington sporting rifle in the saddle sheath.

'You must go back,' said Saul.

She shook her head.

'No, Saul Powers, I am going to see this through. I had wanted to get the old man away—I suppose you realise he is old and probably a bit crazy—but I also wanted to protect you. I cannot explain it, but I have a strange feeling that you will be in great danger. Do not argue. I love you, and that gives me the right to come.'

'You are blackmailing me,' Saul cried in anger. 'You know I will not leave you in the desert, an' you think I won't shoot Jesse Nathan in front of you. But you are wrong. I don't care if you see it.'

He turned and rode back along the trail to where Yellow Dog and the Professor were waiting.

'Come on,' he snapped. 'Let's get movin'.'

Seeing the expression on Saul's face, the Professor said nothing.

'Very soon we see Señor Nathan,' said Yellow Dog, tugging at the burro's lead.

The small party moved forward, Rachel following a few yards behind the Professor. The rest of the journey was made in silence except for Yellow Dog occasionally muttering to himself in Ute.

\* \* \*

Jesse Nathan gazed down at the excavation at the base of the pink bluff. There was no doubt about it! After all these years he had made a strike. His dream had come true. Tears dimmed his faded eyes as he looked at the bright fragments in the heavy palm of his hand. Now he was repaid for his years in the wilderness with its danger, heat and lousy food.

It was also a justification of his faith – the only faith he'd ever known – that somewhere in the Painted Desert there was a seam of gold waiting for him. And now he'd found it, maybe only just in time.

A celebration was in order. Taking up his old carbine and his pick, he climbed a sandy slope to his tattered tent before which the ashes of his breakfast fire still smouldered. He dived into the tent and reappeared with a bottle of Old Vermont. Uncorking it, he sat down in the shade of a large rock.

He took a pull at the bottle which he had kept for months for this very occasion. Again he examined the pieces of raw gold, smiling at the pieces of gleaming metal to which he had dedicated the latter part of his life. In a cracked voice he began to sing an old miner's refrain.

> *There's thirst in the desert*
> *And death in the sun,*
> *But gold there's awaiting*
> *To be found and won.*
>
> *So on with your pack, boy,*
> *And off to your mine,*
> *And search for those nuggets*
> *Which glitter so fine.*
>
> *For there's many a gambler,*
> *And many a game,*
> *Just waiting to swallow*
> *The gold from your claim.*
>
> *And there's many a lady*
> *Whose smile is not cold*
> *For the men who come back*
> *A-laden with gold.*
>
> *But remember the miner*
> *Who's left his poor bones*
> *A-laying a-scattered*
> *On the hot desert stones.*
>
> *For there's thirst in the desert*

*And death in the sun,*
*And you pay with your life*
*For the gold you have won.*

When he looked up he saw a group of people on the rocky ground opposite him. At the top of a low ridge a girl sat like a statue on a horse. By her lounged Yellow Dog, holding the lead of his burro. On a rock sat a tall, flabby man with a long cigar. Closer at hand stood a slim young man with near white hair and blue eyes. Looking at him through the column of heat which rose from the remains of the fire he appeared to tremble as though he was not quite real. With a weary sigh the old man rose to his feet.

'You Jesse Nathan?' Saul demanded.

Nathan blinked in the fierce light, his eyes on the bone-handled Colt Frontier strapped low on the young man's thigh.

Tm Nathan,' he said. 'Reckon you must be Saul Powers.'

Saul nodded bleakly.

'Reckon you come to kill me,' continued the prospector calmly. 'Waal, I can't do anythin' about that. I ain't got no gun except that old carbine.' He pointed to where it lay. 'I ain't a gunfighter no more. So let's get it over with. At least I'm glad you weren't a few hours sooner, I'd never have struck pay dirt.'

'How did you know it was me?' Saul asked.

'It figures, boy. Guess it ain't no secret 'bout the way you've been huntin' down the men what killed your old man. I read about it in some magazine last time I was in San Juan. Figured then that sooner or later you'd catch up with me. There's just one thing I'd like to ask you.'

'Say on.'

'Have you asked anyone – any of the guys you've gone after – why they killed your father?'

'No,' answered Saul, a puzzled look on his face.

Jesse Nathan laughed.

'So you been ridin' out to avenge a crime you don't know a blamed thing about.'

'All right,' said Saul. 'Why did you shoot my father?'

' 'Cause he was a dirty traitor,' the old man replied coldly. 'At that time we were runnin' rustled cattle from the Mexican ranches, or wherever we could get 'em, to the minin' towns up north. We were gettin' blamed good money, them miners were sure hungry.

'There were nine of us, an' the only thing that could have stopped us runnin' the beeves through would have been a good lawman. But there weren't a good lawman, only your father. Sure he was handy with a gun, an' he had everyone's confidence, but he was corrupt, d'ya hear, boy, corrupt! He was takin' a big share of the money we got to let us drive the cattle through without hindrance.'

There was a dazed expression on Saul's features as he regarded the ragged old man.

'Sure, you look surprised, son, but he was in it as much as us. Then there was a mighty big reward offered for us, an' your old man decided to earn it, an' add to his reputation as a law officer. So he tipped off the vigilantes. Only something went wrong with their plans. They struck too soon, an' only got four of us. The rest rode over to your father's place. Guess he didn't know what had happened so he didn't expect trouble. I reckon you know the rest. After that we split up. Ain't never seen the others again.'

'You're lyin', you've got to be lyin',' Saul muttered. 'Tell him he's lyin', Professor.'

The big man shrugged.

'It just doesn't matter any more,' he said.

'By God it does,' shouted Saul. 'It matters to me.

Tell the truth, old man, or I'll kill you.'

'Reckon you aim to anyways,' he replied. 'So why should I lie!'

Saul rubbed his hand across his face.

'Sit down, old man. I ain't gonna hurt you.'

There was a silence. Jesse Nathan slowly eased himself back into the shadow.

'I guess this is the end of the trail,' Saul said as though thinking aloud. 'I guess it was the wrong trail all the time an' I never knew it.'

'What are you talking about?' demanded the Professor. 'Don't get squeamish now. Shoot him.'

'An unarmed old man like this?' said Saul.

'What does it matter. He had no mercy on your father.'

'Like you said, that doesn't matter anymore.'

'Powers, I'm telling you to shoot him, I'll say he drew first in the papers, but you've got to kill him. Everythin' we've worked for comes to nothin' unless you complete the quest.'

Saul shook his head and turned away from the prospector.

'Powers, kill him or I'll shoot you!' The Professor held his derringer in his hand. 'I've made you what you are; a top gun, a man who inspires fear and respect. I've given you sweet revenge. Now you've got to give me something. Turn round and shoot Jesse Nathan, otherwise I will not hesitate to use this gun. I made you, and I can destroy you.'

'So, you've pulled a gun on me, Professor,' said Saul sadly. 'You must be loco. You ain't got a chance against me with that toy. You're facing a gun-fighter, Professor, a gunfighter you created your self...'

'I'm going to count to three, Powers,' the Professor said. Before he could begin Saul's hand dropped to his holster. The derringer wavered as he leapt forward, gun in hand. But the shot never came from the Frontier. Instead it swept in an arc at the end of Saul's arm and the barrel struck the Professor on the side of the head, leaving a crimson weal.

The Derringer fell to the ground. The Professor rocked in agony. The terrible impact of the sharp barrel had knocked off his spectacles and now fragments of blue glass sparkled like sapphires in the sand.

'A few minutes ago I'd have killed you,' said Saul. 'But I ain't got the stomach no more. Take back the gun you gave me.' He threw the Frontier at the Professor's feet.

'I hope you write this up for the *Frontier Journal*,' he said bitterly. 'You could call it "The End of a Gun-fighter".'

The Professor took no notice, but continued to moan. The whole side of his face was now covered with blood.

Saul began to walk towards Rachel. As he did so Jesse Nathan leaned over and picked up his carbine. Calmly he aimed at the retreating man and squeezed the trigger. The bullet grazed Saul's shoulder.

He spun round to see the old man work the lever of the gun and take aim again.

'I reckon you shoulda taken your pal's advice,' said Nathan as he squinted at Saul along the barrel. 'Now it's too late. I'm gonna drop you, son. If I didn't the' day might come when you'd change your mind an' come after me again.'

Saul looked at the ragged figure with the carbine. He felt he had never been closer to death. His gun arm tensed, but there was no gun to reach for. All he could do was wait for eternity.

Next instant there was the crack of a rifle...and Jesse Nathan toppled forward across the embers of his fire.

Saul turned and walked to Rachel who held her smoking Remington. When he reached her he gently took the gun and placed it in its sheath. Then he took the reins of his horse and swung into the saddle.

'It's all over, Rachel,' he said, 'Let's go.' She nodded as though coming out of a trance.

'Get your Colt,' she said.

He shook his head.

'That's all behind me now.'

'Yellow Dog, please bring that gun,' she ordered. The Indian obeyed, handing it to Saul.'

'You are still Saul Powers,' Rachel said. 'You may not want to be a gun-fighter any more, but that doesn't end your reputation. Somewhere, someday, someone is going to want that reputation. You must be able to defend yourself.'

'Yeah,' said Saul. 'It's somethin' I guess you just can't live down.' He bolstered the Frontier.

The girl smiled slightly, and the warm breeze carried a strand of her long hair across her face. Ignoring the Professor who was slumped with his head in his hands, they began to canter back along the track between the twisted rock formations. The hoofbeats of their horses faded. Soon the trail was empty save for the drifting tumble-weed.